Anna Lavrinenko (b. 1984) lives in Yaroslavl (Central Russia). A Law graduate she works as a company lawyer in Yaroslavl as well as taking an active part in the city's cultural life: she leads a reading group there and reviews books and films for the local press. Her short stories and essays have been published in the top literary and art magazines. Her *L'enfant perdu* came out in French from L'Aube in 2013.

Winner of the Debut Prize in 2006, Lavrinenko follows the tradition of the great 19th-century Russian literature.

Lavrinenko is in love with her native city of Yaroslavl where all her stories take place. But apart from the ancient cathedrals she shows you the nooks and crannies you'll never find in any travel guides: the real adventure begins where the touristy trail ends.

GLAS NEW RUSSIAN WRITING

contemporary Russian literature

in English translation

Volume 62

This is the twelfth
volume in the Glas
sub-series devoted to
winners and finalists
of the Debut Prize.
Glas acknowledges the
support of the Debut
Prize in publishing this
book.

ANNA LAVRINENKO

Yaroslavl Stories

**Translated by Christopher Tauchen
and Amanda Love Darragh**

GLAS PUBLISHERS
tel: +7(495)441-9157
perova@glas.msk.su
www.glas.msk.su

DISTRIBUTION

In North America
Consortium Book Sales and Distribution
tel: 800-283-3572; fax: 800-351-5073
orderentry@perseusbooks.com
www.cbsd.com

In the UK
CENTRAL BOOKS
orders@centralbooks.com
www.centralbooks.com
Direct orders: INPRESS
tel: 0191 229 9555   .
customerservices@inpressbooks.co.uk
www.inpressbooks.co.uk

Within Russia
Jupiter-Impex
www.jupiterbooks.ru

Editors: Natasha Perova & Joanne Turnbull
Camera-ready copy: Tatiana Shaposhnikova

Front cover photographs: Alena Lukashenko, *Church of St Elijah the Prophet,*
    and Ilya Tikhanovsky, *Young Crowd.*
Half-titles: Vasily Merzlyakov, *Yaroslavl Winter.*

ISBN 978-5-7172-0126-1

CONTENTS

Author's Note

I think of this book as a "provincial saga." Love-stricken adolescents, young people in search of their place in the world, the story of a young rock band, a parable of a man who suddenly discovers his strength and a will to live that had long been lost, legends of the old theater – at first glance these stories do not appear to have much in common, but each of them is in some way connected to my native city of Yaroslavl located in Central Russia, 200 miles from Moscow. My characters all walk the same streets and visit the same places. Their lives touch one another and intersect in the most intricate ways. One of my characters says: "Everyone knows everyone else here, and you always know someone who knows someone who knows you. You go out with your friend's ex-girlfriend. It's a closed circle. A big village."

I was born and raised in Yaroslavl. To tourists, it's a historic Russian city dating back a thousand years. In the guidebooks you can find the attractions of the old town center, a UNESCO World Heritage Site: the towers of the Yaroslavl kremlin, countless churches, cathedrals, and ancient monasteries. The embankment along the Volga leads you past the domed pavilions, which have long been an unofficial symbol of the city, to the Strelka, a triangular plot at the confluence of the Volga, Europe's longest river, and its tributary, the Kotorosl. We are proud that the first official Russian theatre was founded in Yaroslavl, and it's a shame to see its decay today, both the art and the building itself.

If you go a bit out of your way, you can find another Yaroslavl, a major industrial center. The world's first synthetic rubber works was built here, also Russia's first oil refinery, and much else. The manufacturing firms on the city's outskirts do their best to pollute the air and stimulate the local economy.

However, my characters and I live in a completely different Yaroslavl. This is the everyday Yaroslavl, the one that is part and parcel of our consciousness. We do not stop to admire the Church of St. Elijah the Prophet. We do not stroll along the Volga embankment to view the historical panorama. There are many things that go unseen by tourists, but which we notice and love. Crossing the Kotorosl River early on a winter morning, we observe fearless anglers sitting out on fragile ice. We love our hockey team: nearly everyone is a fan. In 2011, when the team was killed in a plane crash, it was a tragedy for the entire city. We even love our unfinished Chaika Hotel standing there in the center of the city for more than twenty years now. We love our local catchwords and sayings, which are incomprehensible to people even from the neighboring regions. This is the city I write about in my stories.

My characters are provincials – for them, time flows just a bit slower than it does for people in the capital. But their problems are no simpler or less significant. They have the same joys and sorrows as anyone else. My intention as the author was to introduce readers to this special world of my Yaroslavl. And I hope after reading this book you'll come to love my city.

Lost and Found

LOST AND FOUND

1

She lost me in an airport. Many years later I grew up. But then I was a small boy of about five or a bit younger, wearing a little red hoodie, gray corduroys, brown boots that had been carefully laced by his mother, with a blue cap and a little kangaroo backpack, sitting in the chair with his legs swinging back and forth as they still didn't reach the floor and he could kick them however much he wanted. An ordinary little boy in no way different from other boys his age, except that someone had lost him. This boy turned into me.

I am a man of about thirty, about 180 cm tall, with short blond hair, blue eyes, pale thin lips – an ordinary man, in no way different from other men his age, except that a long time ago someone lost him in an airport.

She said: "Sit here and don't go anywhere. I'll be back soon." I nodded. I believed her because she was my mother and I was just a little boy.

She said: "I won't lose you." And she kissed me on the cheek.

I still hear those words: I won't lose you I won't lose you I won't lose you won't lose you won't lose you iwon'tloseyouwon'tloseyou *I – won't – lose – you*. But I don't believe them anymore.

She said: "I won't lose you." And she kissed me on the cheek.

Those pale thin lips that articulated this lie, those blue eyes (just like mine), that long blond hair – these are my first childhood memories.

She tossed a duffle bag over her shoulder and walked away without looking back: no parting glance, no blowing kisses, no apologetic half-smile. My mother didn't really know how to express her feelings.

I'm not sure how much time had passed before I worked out that she wasn't coming back: maybe a few minutes, hours, an entire night or day. I was hungry. I pulled out the slightly melted chocolate bar from one of the front pockets of my backpack, tore open the wrapper, and wolfed it down. I wiped my dirty hands on my trousers. My mother usually wiped them with a tissue – "Dirty again?" – but she wasn't there, so my hands remained sticky. After that, it seems, I nodded off. I'm not sure that I managed to sleep much. I still felt hungry and I was worried that my mother wasn't coming back. All around were men's and women's voices, the cries of children, and the sounds of airplanes tearing away from the earth, When I opened my eyes it seemed that another day had begun, as if it had been Monday, and now it was Tuesday. Maybe I really did sleep that long.

Then the time came to be frightened and panic for real, and I burst into tears. My mother never came back. She was the first woman in my life who abandoned me.

You may not think much of me for wallowing in self-pity, needing the consolation of tears, for asking for – no, more like demanding – your sympathy. Think what you want: I was just a little boy! Don't grown-ups know that you can't abandon small children at the airport and not come back for them?

There were two of them. She said:
"Look! What a darling little boy! Is he all alone?"
There were two of them, and they were looking at me.

Her: medium height, stout, wearing pink lipstick. Not a beauty, but still not so bad.

Him: a good bit taller than her and skinny (it looked like you could fold him in two), a pair of sad gray eyes looking out of brown-framed glasses, and thin stubble on his chin.

"Hello, child!" she said in a tiny little voice; it was immediately clear that she was up to something.

The man set a hand on her shoulder:

"Come on now, it's none of your business!"

"But he might be lost," she barked at him. "Are you lost, child?" Again with the kiddy voice.

I shook my head no.

"Where is your mother, child?"

Even though her idiotic habit of calling me "child" was getting on my nerves, I shrugged: wouldn't I like to know.

"Did she leave?"

I nodded.

"You poor child!"

She sat down in the chair next to me and placed her hand on the back of my head. Her sparkly pink mouth appeared before me: I could see her crooked white teeth and red tongue.

"And you're here all on your own?"

"Let's go already, we're late for our flight." The man looked at his watch and then at some distant place where, apparently, the "flight" was.

"Shut up, you! He doesn't have anybody." She said this so I wouldn't hear, but I heard it anyway.

"So what?"

"He's been abandoned, he's got no one! We can't leave him all alone! We should take him home!"

"What? Are you crazy!" He was pointing to his temple and twisting his wrist.

"Shut up and hear me out." She spoke in whispers with her hand still on my head. She whispered something to him very quietly. I could have heard if I'd wanted to, but I didn't, it was all the same to me. I was upset and angry at my mother. I missed her and didn't give a damn about anything else.

When he finally gave in and said, "All right, then," she smiled and whispered "I love you." I thought she was saying those words to the man, but then I noticed out of the corner of my eye that she had been looking at me. I took an immediate dislike to those three words: they were empty, pointless, meaningless. Long ago someone played a cruel joke by starting the rumor that those words were very important and that they meant something serious, even though they really mean nothing at all...

I've said them too: not because I believe them or understand what they mean, but because that's just what people do. I said those words to my wife because she smiled when she heard them, and I said them to other women when I wanted sex or when saying it was unavoidable. I didn't want to mislead anyone; I was just doing what everyone does.

Those two, the woman with the pink lipstick and the man with the sad gray eyes, took me from that waiting room and became my new parents, and from then on they would never tell me the truth.

When I was little I often asked about her, about my real mother, but they told me that I'd made it all up. You've never had another mother. There never was any woman with long blond hair and blue eyes. There was no airport. No one lost you. By the time I was an adult I realized that they were never going to tell me about my real mother and that I didn't really care, so I quit asking them about it. I never thought about looking for her, and I nearly stopped thinking about her altogether.

And now, as I found myself on an empty landing in the stairwell of my apartment building, I thought about her and everything else in my confused and senseless life, and it felt like I was right back there, in the airport, still waiting for something.

One day you leave your apartment for a five-minute cigarette run and you forget your keys on the hall table. The door slams shut, and you realize you're not getting back in. And then you sit down on the stairs, light your last cigarette, and for some reason start searching for the meaning of life.

I pressed my forehead against the cold wall, double-checked my pockets, as if the keys might appear by magic, and listened. The elevator didn't move for a long time. The entire stairwell, or at least what I could hear of it, was silent. Maybe no one was home. They were at work, or at school, or out walking their dogs: everyone doing their usual thing, which is what I'd have been doing if it hadn't been for that door. All of a sudden I wanted to be on my own sofa with some cigarettes and the remote control.

But instead I had to go. Probably to someone else's place, anywhere I might find a spare set of keys to this stupid door. And no matter how much I wanted to, I couldn't sit here all day on this cold step feeling sorry for myself.

2

Turn your right arm, head, and body to the side – *one* – now back with the left arm, head, and body – *two* – let your legs do their own thing, and now drop your arms – *three* – back straight, stand on tiptoe, don't let your heels touch the floor! And again, one last time: turn with your head, turn with your whole body, your right arm, head, body this way – *one* – and back with left arm, head, body – *two* – let the legs do their own thing, then both arms drop – *three*. They're still standing on tiptoe: their heels have no desire to touch the floor. *One, two, three, one, two, three* – and again – *one, two, three*.

I could never get tired of watching her dance: she is the most beautiful woman I have ever seen.

The music stopped abruptly on some note. I never studied music, so I couldn't say which one. She stopped dancing at the same time.

"Thanks, everyone," she said. She was standing in third position: heels together, toes apart. "We'll see you at the next session on Monday."

"Bye!" answered a jumbled chorus of seven- and eight-year old girls.

Small and serious, wearing identical black long-sleeved shirts and translucent white skirts, the girls left the studio one by one, keeping their slim shoulders straight, heads held high, and crossing the wooden floor in their cream ballet flats. The most beautiful dancer, standing with her back to me, was putting a glittering CD back into its case. I could see the outline of her elegant, fragile shoulder blades under her white T-shirt; her dark hair was tied up with a hairpin, exposing the freckled back of her neck, where a few unruly curls danced back and forth.

"What are you doing here?" she asked without turning around.

"I missed you," I answered.

She turned toward me and rubbed her forehead. I noticed that she looked worn out: a few more lines on her face, dark bags under her eyes. But no: she hadn't aged at all. She was just a bit older.

"Did something happen again?" she asked.

"Nothing happened. Do I need a reason to visit my wife?"

"Ex-wife."

"Same thing."

I sat down. Some people came in, but I didn't see who because I was sitting with my back to them.

"Are you leaving?" A woman's tired voice, just like my wife's.

"Not yet, I'll still be a little while."

"All right. Will you lock up?

"Yes, of course."

All the mirrors in the studio reflected her image: thin, pale, tired. Her reflection said: "Tell me what you're here for. You never come just because."

I didn't answer the reflection's question. I was looking in the mirror, not at my wife.

"You seem tired. Been working a lot?"

She came and sat in the chair next to me. I couldn't stop looking at her reflection next to that other man. That man wasn't me. I didn't know him and hadn't ever seen him before: the week-old beard, the savage appearance, those thin knees under faded jeans, and that worn gray sweater that looks two sizes too big. It can't be me, it's someone else entirely.

I took her hand and squeezed it tight. She used to be my wife, and now we were only reflections in the mirrors of an empty dance studio, long divorced.

We were young and deliriously happy when we got married. I put the ring on her finger and thought that nothing could break us apart. Three years later we were divorced.

Back then we were renting a tiny apartment where the hot water and heating would often go out and the only furniture we owned was a disintegrating sofa and a TV with three channels. What were we thinking when we got married? You see, when people get married young, without so much as a ruble in their pockets or any decent prospects, renting a pathetic apartment in the worst area of town, these people aren't thinking at all! But here's the strange thing: none of that affected our relationship. We may have been complete failures, but we were happy: somehow I'd manage not to notice when we were having noodles for the fourth night in a row. And sure, I know that to some extent I'm idealizing that life and our relationship, but I'd prefer to think it really was like that. Then at least I can know that I was happy at some point and that I managed to make someone else happy even if it only happened once.

I waited for her every day after work: I'd sit in this very dance studio and watch her teach the girls how to move elegantly and maintain their posture. When her last session finished at nine we'd go buy something for dinner and head home. Being happy seemed simple to me then. It never occurred to me that anyone could live differently. I didn't really believe my friends when they complained about having fights with their wives; I'd just shrug when I learned that yet another one of them was getting a divorce.

For us the trouble started after a year of this happy life. We didn't want to admit that anything was wrong, so we never tried to deal with it. Perhaps this was simpler, and we didn't really need each other anymore. I stopped meeting her after work, and she stopped falling asleep on my shoulder. She started going out with friends more often: they never invited me, and I never asked to come. Unhappy and bored, I got to know a neighbor woman from upstairs, two or three times.

I still can't work out how my wife found out. Maybe the woman gave me away, or maybe I let on somehow, secretly hoping to be caught. She wouldn't tell me how she found out or why she didn't make a big deal of it before.

Our decision to get divorced was quick and unplanned, just like our decision to get married. We got spectacularly drunk afterwards. I opened a bottle of wine, then another. We smoked a lot.

She said: "I think something's wrong. We haven't had sex in two months, and it seems like neither of us really wants to, at least not with each other. We don't do anything together, and the last time we talked was last week when we had to decide what kind of toothpaste to get."

I said: "There's nothing wrong with us. It's just a rough patch, but it will be over soon."

She said: "I know about the neighbor."

There was a long silence, and then I started to defend myself – "It was just sex." – and attack her – "Why didn't you bring this up when you found out, like a normal person?"

She said: "I don't know. I really wanted everything with us to work out."

Then she said: "But all the same I can't stop thinking about it, because it's not easy to imagine the person you live with fucking someone else."

The person you live with. Not the person you *love*. This was no slip of the tongue. She knew full well what she was saying, and now things felt a lot worse. All the same, my belief in that word remains low.

I didn't answer her for a long time. I just didn't know what to say. What is there to say? The standard "I love you" wouldn't work, and "I need you" would sound mocking.

I asked: "What do we do now?"

She answered: "I have no idea."

Then we both cried. We didn't know what was going to happen, but we understood that it couldn't go on like this. She suggested that we separate. I agreed because I knew that it would be easier, not for me, but for her, and I also understood that it wouldn't be just a long separation: this would be permanent.

I kept visiting her at the dance studio. I'd go when I just couldn't take it anymore, when something in my life wasn't right. I'd come here as I had before, when I went every day to watch her dance, and at the end of the lesson she'd say to the girls "Thanks, everyone. See you next time."

We – no, not us, but our reflections – were in the empty dance studio. We were older. We had changed. Somewhere along the way we'd lost hope and abandoned our dreams, though we tried not to think about it. We'd wasted our lives on something insubstantial, on something unimportant, and we'd forgotten how to be happy.

Her cold hand was in mine. I really wished I could warm her up.

"What am I going to do with you?" Her voice was tired and sad.

"I wish I knew." My reflection shrugged awkwardly.

Suddenly I realized that she was exhausted. She wanted to get home, shower, eat, and go to bed, but instead she was here, sitting quietly with a specter from her past in an empty dance studio, not taking her hand away from mine. I didn't want to keep her any longer.

"I got locked out of my apartment. Did I ever give you a spare set of keys?"

"I knew it. I knew something happened!"

"It was an accident, really. I went out, closed the door, and completely forgot about the keys. Funny, isn't it?"

"Very. You're thirty years old! When are you going to grow up?"

"So does that mean you don't have a set?"

"No, I don't have anything! You've got to know you can't go on living like this!"

"Don't tell me how to live my life – you're the one who ran off, who left me. And who said you wouldn't lose me?"

"Bullshit. First of all, I never said that, and second, I'm not the one who ran away – you're the one who was always going upstairs for a quick fuck."

"As it happens, it wasn't always that quick."

To my surprise, she started laughing. This was one of the things I always liked about her: she didn't take offence at all the stupid things I said.

"Sorry, that was…"

"Still making those awful jokes? I still can't get mad at you for that. You've always been that way. Unfit for real life.

Seems like you live in your own world, where they've no room for me."

We were holding hands. I was desperate to warm her cold hands. They were always like that. I wanted to kiss her but knew that I couldn't. I was sorry that things had turned out this way.

"I'd better be going." I got up from my chair.

"Wait." Her voice was softer. I must've looked even more miserable.

"What?"

"I love you." She hugged me. "You're going to be just fine!"

"I know, I know," I said, but I didn't really know that at all. I was used to her talking to me like she did, constantly reassuring me that I was going to be just fine.

3

If only I could remember where they were! But I couldn't. I didn't know if there even were any spare keys.

So now I had to go somewhere to look for them. All so I could get back into an apartment that I really didn't want to get back into.

Home, sweet home! Yeah, right.

It's not that I cared very much about the apartment itself: I just needed somewhere to sleep. Just imagine: the small pink flowers on what was once white wallpaper, now yellowed by God-knows-what; the squeaky worn-out sofa bed, which I folded back into a sofa only on holidays; the sheets, reeking of tobacco smoke; the fifteen-channel TV; the maddening curtainless windows that let in the morning sun; books stacked on the floor because there was no bookcase; the bare light bulbs that I replaced only when all three had gone out – if the apartment itself meant anything to me at all, then something was seriously wrong.

I was at a loss where else to go and so I went to work. The office wasn't far, just a ten-minute walk, which was probably the only good thing about the job. I never dreamed of doing what I do. I could have been anything: a CEO or a famous guitarist, one of those rich kids that waste their parents' money and their own lives, or a successful attorney who locks up drug addicts, or maybe a doctor, a wine taster, or a bank robber – I could have done anything but this. Sure, it could have been worse, but that's not what happened. It turned out the way it did, and that was that. No one bothered to ask whether I liked it.

I became a mediocre employee in the commercial sector.

I worked in the consumer hotline division of a major company that has branches spread all across Russia. I don't want to give it extra publicity – good or bad – so I'm not going to say which one. The company itself was enormous, and our office was just a small part of the whole, and I was an even smaller part of that small part, whatever that is. And what was this consumer hotline all about? Don't you remember? Yes, of course you do. We're the ones that ran that ad campaign: *If you are not satisfied with our product or if it does not bring the desired effect, call our consumer hotline and we will give you a full refund.* People called all the time, but we never gave anyone a refund.

I answered people's calls: complaints, queries, requests, suggestions. Every month I wrote a report for management that no one ever read. With the mark of a connoisseur I discussed milk products, new cheese varieties, and yogurt flavors, even though I'd never tried them and never planned to.

My work was boring and pointless, and it did no one any good: not me, not the company, and not our customers.

The hotline callers could be divided into three types:

Type 1: the well-meaning ones. All they wanted to find

out was whether they could give yogurt to children with pollen allergies. Even when they were dissatisfied with my answer, or if I showed myself to be completely incompetent, to my embar… (actually, no, that didn't bother me at all), or if I said, "Although you consumed our product and it did not bring the desired effect, unfortunately we cannot give you a refund." And then I would repeat one of the universal reasons that our company had come up with to deal with similar cases – these kinds of people would still say "thank you" (why? for lying to them? for the pleasant conversation? because I couldn't give them an intelligent response to their query? – who knows), wish me a good day, and always wait for me to hang up first.

Type 2: people who were eternally dissatisfied with life. They swore, yelled into the receiver, demanded refunds, asked to speak with a manager, and threatened to sue. But so far none of them had actually followed through. Sometimes one of them would call repeatedly over the course of a day, a week, or a month. After three or four months of persistent calling and a final "I've already filed my lawsuit," the calls would stop. I understand these people, to some extent. They were dissatisfied with their lives, probably like I was with mine. They vented their anger in any way they could: some kicked their pets, some beat their wives, and the more cerebral types would call the consumer hotline of this or some other company. I'm not joking.

Type 3: people who just wanted to talk. It's true, these people do exist. Sometimes they'd call more than once, and we'd become good friends on the phone. We'd ask about one another's health not out of politeness, but genuinely, because we really wanted to know about the other person's life. I knew the names of their dogs, what color wallpaper they'd put up in their kitchen, what their grandchildren did for a living. They knew what I'd had for lunch and the name of my next-door neighbor, and how much I earned by talking to them for a living. When it comes down to it, I'm just like them, though I'm sometimes reluctant to admit it.

I had never met someone who I could call a colleague because I had never known anyone with a job quite like mine. They don't teach it in any university or school. Sometimes I found myself thinking about someone working the hotline elsewhere in our company, or maybe the hotline of a similar company. Where would this person be? Maybe he was in New York, looking down from his skyscraper, looking at the other skyscrapers and the sparkling snow, which always covers the ground in angled figures, never circles. Maybe he was in some other city – Tokyo, Paris, London, Madrid – leafing through a glossy magazine about gold watches. Or maybe he was in a squat in Rome ordering a pizza. Maybe he was eating Chinese in front of the TV in Toronto. Does it make a difference what he was wearing? An Armani suit or torn jeans and an orange T-shirt? Did he have a girlfriend, or did he date a new girl every night? I mean, was he as much of a loser as I was, or had life been better to him? Now that I think of it, maybe he wasn't a man at all, but a woman.

I'd been working for this company for several years already. At first I assumed it would be only for a few months. Who could take this kind of work seriously? But the pay wasn't bad, and I thought that in a year or so I could trade it in for something better: I would become successful, satisfied with my life and my job. But then, well... Never make the mistake I made. Don't take a job you don't like, even if you think that it's temporary, that it's "only for a few months." I'd fallen into a trap that I still couldn't get out of. In the beginning I really did try to find something else, even if without much enthusiasm. I managed to blow off interviews, or something unexpected would keep me from going, or I would end up going but find something not quite right with the place, or the employer would find something not quite right with me.

Anyway, I was glad of one thing: the reason I never got an interesting job wasn't because I turned one down, but because nothing I found was any better than what I was already doing. There was no point in moving from one bad job to another. So I stayed put.

Fortunately, the office was open. Timur, one of the managers, was smoking outside.

"It's good you're still here. I needed to drop in to see if I left my spare keys in my desk."

"I was just about to leave," he said. "But what's a few minutes? Go ahead and look for your keys. We'll lock up when you're done. God knows why we've got to lock up. Maybe they think there's something worth stealing? The computers aren't fit to be sold for scrap, and we've never had anything more valuable than that."

Timur stayed on the front steps, and I went to my work station: an ordinary desk facing a wall at the back of a tiny room; an ancient wreck of a computer; a telephone, which depressingly reminded me of Soviet times and made me crave a shiny new cordless phone, silver with orange buttons and loads of unnecessary functions; a couple of files with last year's reports; and a folder with caricatures drawn by a programmer who quit last year and bequeathed me the pleasure of seeing our superiors with enormous heads and beer bellies.

Even though I'd been working there the longest, my desk was in no way personalized: no pictures or porcelain dogs or any of the other knickknacks that people decorate their desks with. All I needed to work well was a cup of hot tea and a pen and paper, which I would use for doodling while half-listening to customers instead of writing down their complaints, requests, and suggestions. Who really cares?

One after another I went through the drawers of my so-called *work*-station.

In the first: two tea bags, three dried-up pens, old checks, crumpled-up papers, two candy wrappers. No spare keys.

In the second: ads for our products – they send these to us from headquarters with detailed descriptions of new items set for release, the usual nonsense that I'm supposed to tell callers and that I never read. Still no keys.

In the third: a stack of cards, given to me at different times by various coworkers. Cards for New Year's, birthdays, Army Day, a few prank Valentines. I was never in the mood to do anything with them; many of the people who gave them to me had been gone a long time, and I didn't even know where they were now. There was also a picture of my wife that I never looked at: I never opened this drawer, so the keys couldn't be there. And they weren't.

I took a deep breath. My life was in these drawers, everything was there. My life was a complete waste of time. I wasn't doing it right, not quite living properly, this couldn't be right. I used to think this was how it was meant to be. But what if it wasn't? What if I was just a coward, wallowing in self-pity? A coward, too scared to leave my job and start doing something worthwhile. A coward, afraid of falling in love, who thought he was too old for love and that anyone he might fall in love with would leave him. A coward, afraid of asking his parents for the truth about his real mother, about the airport where she left him. A coward who not once tried to find her. Pathetic. Half my life wasted. There was a time when I believed I would make something of myself: I was eighteen or nineteen and thought that I had all the time in the world. But time didn't give a damn about my hopes and dreams. Why should it care about me? It passed me by without acknowledging my presence, and I did nothing, achieved nothing. My wife was right: I was entirely unfit for real life.

I grabbed a fresh sheet of paper and a pen and wrote my letter of resignation, just like that. If nothing came of it, if I didn't manage to start a new life, there would always be a way out: you can always get by on unemployment benefits and odd jobs, or eke out a miserable existence living with your parents, go hitchhiking, marry a rich old woman, sleep in train stations, go back to your old job, shoot yourself, go insane – the exits are many. If it doesn't work out, then you've got options, whatever you like best. It had to be worth the attempt. Why not? It's not like it could get any worse.

4

Things never turn out as you expect. No matter how much you consider all the possibilities, you're bound to overlook the one that eventually takes place.

My wife and I thought that our marriage would last forever, but it didn't. It was the same with my friends. Over the years we grew apart. When you no longer have time for sports and bars, or for discussing women, new computer games, albums, and films, friendships tend to fade away.

But maybe I was just imagining things, and our friendship was the same as it ever was. So why didn't we see each other more often? The measure of a friendship is not the quantity, but the quality of the time spent together. This may be the case, which was why I went to see Gennady.

There was no chance of him having my keys, but still I needed some proof, not just of that, but also of the strength of our friendship. I needed to know that there was something I could count on.

Gennady was home. He didn't seem surprised to see me, almost as if I dropped in on him every day. I was glad to see this.

"Come on in!" he said.

His wife came out from the other room and greeted me with genuine interest in how I was doing. I always liked that woman.

Gennady had changed. He was heavier now, and his hair was beginning to go gray. No more novelty T-shirts. He gave the impression that he was constantly exhausted. He kept rubbing his eyes and forehead, but perhaps this was because of the lighting. Maybe I didn't look any better, especially this evening. How long had it been? Looked like at least a few years. How could that be? We must have seen one another at someone's birthday party or some other celebration. I tried to remember, but there was nothing.

"Come on, then," said Gennady as he put on his coat.

"Where are we going?"

"Come on, you'll see…"

"I didn't know there was a new Chinese restaurant around here."

"Yeah, hasn't been long now. Which means it's still good and cheap. But then they'll start raising the rent."

"Of course," I said stuffing myself with chicken.

The awkwardness had begun to subside. Perhaps it would disappear entirely once we'd had enough beer. That's how it always is: alcohol makes it easier for people to understand one another. Maybe people ought to keep themselves in a constant state of peaceful inebriation. Then the entire world might reach a state of mutual understanding.

"Seems like you've had a rough day," Gennady said.

I was surprised. How'd he know? I hadn't said anything about the keys, but even if I had, forgetting your keys isn't that big of a deal.

We talked about nothing, just like before.

He said:

"I've seen your wife here."

"Ex-wife."

"Whatever. She looks tired."

"I know. I went to see her today."

"You did? What for?"

"Keys. I thought I might've given her a spare set."

"And?"

"And what?"

"Did she have any?"

"No. I don't suppose I left them with you, did I?"

"No, I never got any. What happened?"

"I locked myself out."

"You locked yourself out?"

"Yeah."

For some time we sat there in silence, but it wasn't awkward at all. We could have stayed like that for hours without asking ourselves that torturous question: "What should I say?"

"You can stay with me tonight, if you want. We've got a spare bed."

"Thanks, but no. I think I'll go to my parents' place and see if they've got my keys. My mother knows I'm a bit absent-minded, probably had some made herself."

"All right."

We stayed a bit longer. Genka picked up the check, and I didn't fight him. The crumpled wad of cash in my pocket didn't amount to much.

When we said our goodbyes outside his stairwell, I asked him whether he thought we should meet up more often.

"Of course. Now that you're unemployed, you'll have plenty of time for that."

We shook hands, and I set off without knowing where I was going.

"Dima!" he shouted.

I turned around.

"Here!" He tossed me a pack of cigarettes. "You never did get that smoke."

5

Reality has little in common with the imagination. In our dreams we ascribe qualities to people that they themselves are not aware of. They'd be astonished to hear about it, just as you'd be astonished to hear what people actually thought about you. Never fear: sometimes their opinion of you is much better than your own.

Anyway, here's what would happen: I'd be introduced to some girl, and after talking for a couple hours I'd start thinking that I liked her, I wanted her, and then I'd be head-over-heels in love. I'd daydream about her, drawing her image in my mind, imagining the curve of her neck, her delicate wrists, that gorgeous smile. But as soon as I saw her again, she seemed not at all like I'd imagined. I never understood: What did this mean? How could I think I was so madly in love with her, with this perfectly ordinary girl, with this ordinary neck and these ordinary wrists?

Finally I understood: in our fantasies we tend to love people much more than in reality. When two people, middle-aged lovers, say, or a young couple whose parents disapprove of the match, see one another rarely, maybe once every few weeks, they start imagining what the other person is like, and they invent more and more, giving the other one words and actions that were never said or done in real life, and then, when that person doesn't say or do those things, the veil is lifted. Of course, such a situation may never come up, and you might keep attributing to them these words or actions that don't ever happen and have never happened. What it comes down to is this: you've invented this other person. You will think that the only reason they didn't talk like this or behave like that is because they didn't get a chance to. That's all. You don't see one another that often, and the opportunity just didn't arise, right? And if such a situation were to occur, then everything would be just as you imagined, wouldn't it? Of course it would.

What I'm trying to say is this: everything people say about love is nonsense. We just imagine it. Very few of us are capable of loving reality, and the people who can are those who have no imagination whatsoever.

I'm saying all of this so I can answer one simple question, a question whose answer never changes but which I'd like to have answered all the same: Do I love my mother? Not the one who found me, but the one who lost me. Fine, no more lying: not lost, but abandoned. Could I love this woman? All I can actually remember are those blue eyes and long blond hair, nothing more. I can't remember her voice, the way she walked, how she smelled. But I do know what it was like, I imagine it, her image flashing hundreds of times through my mind, constantly moving toward perfection. That's why I never say she abandoned me, why I say that she lost me: this dreamed-up mother loved me, so she would never be capable of abandoning me. Do you know what she'd say if we happened to meet? She'd say: "I'm so sorry, I left for a minute, and when I came back you were gone." Of course, it's more likely she'd say something altogether different. So I don't want to look for her, don't want to spoil the image. I don't want to find out that she's not anything like that. I don't want to find she doesn't smell of coffee and vanilla but rather of some cologne, or that she has some awful dye job and gray roots, or that her eyes are not blue but some kind of lifeless gray. I don't want to know that she actually abandoned me at the airport because she doesn't love me and never did. I don't want to find out that she is no more, that she died. Worst of all would be to find out that she never really existed.

I said that I don't want to look for my mother, and that's true: I don't anymore. But I'd be lying if I said that the thought didn't occur to me. I used to dream of it, thinking about when I found her, how I'd look again into her deep blue eyes and say: "Hello, Mama!" And there was a time when this almost happened. I almost found her. It seems funny now, the absurdity of it, but at the time I wasn't laughing. I wanted to cry like a little boy.

After the divorce I moved into a small apartment. It was even smaller than the one we'd been renting together. The owner was a woman, an acquaintance of my parents. I had met her only twice. The first time was when she showed me the apartment, and the second was when I gave her the rent.

She was about forty-five then, maybe fifty, and she looked very good for her age. Her mental illness, which had just begun to develop, was living inside her and would later manifest itself, transforming this handsome woman into a lunatic who frightened small children.

Here's what happened.

6

"Come inside, come inside, take off your coat. Have a seat in the living room. Care for some tea?"

"None for me, thanks."

"How many sugars?

"Two, please."

After a minute she came back. She placed the small cups on a coffee table and sat down in the chair across from me. She must have been beautiful once, but she had since grown plump and stopped wearing makeup. All the same, she looked good and had a pleasant smell, something like cocoa and cinnamon.

"It's not the end of the month, you know."

"I know. I wanted to pay for two months in advance. While I've got the cash."

"Oh! That's good. That means I've got at least two months until I have to worry about my apartment."

"I always try to be a good tenant."

"And you are. I haven't gotten a single complaint from the neighbors. And Aunt Lusya is quite smitten with you."

"Lusya? The old woman on the second floor?

"That's her."

"I think she's wonderful."

"She thinks the same of you."

The woman smiled. For the first time that evening I was able to relax.

She tucked a strand of hair behind her ear.

I looked around, trying to find signs of someone else living in the apartment.

Was she all alone? There certainly wasn't anyone else living there. Had it always been like that or did she once have a husband or children? The apartment didn't look empty, not like the apartment of a lonely spinster. No cats, no yapping dog, no porcelain figurines, no still-life paintings of fruit. Her apartment looked as if her husband might come in at any moment, give her a big smile, and light up a cigar. And then, out of nowhere, her all but grown-up children would show up and proclaim that their mother is the best in the world.

The silence dragged on as we drank out tea.

"Do you live alone?" I asked.

"Yes."

"Oh. I understand."

"And what exactly do you 'understand'?"

My face went red and I buried my face in my tea.

She said, "My husband died a long time ago."

"I'm sorry. It's none of my business."

"No need to apologize. It's fine."

"Any kids?"

"I'm a terrible mother."

"I don't believe you."

"You will."

There was a silence, and then she spoke again: "I lost him."

"What? You mean… he died?"

"No, he's not dead. I literally lost him, left him for a minute at an airport, and when I got back he was gone."

A shudder went through me and my hands began to quake. I looked at her carefully, examined this woman now appeared to be my mother.

"But how can that be? Is that even possible?"

"You know full well, Dima, it is."

I fell silent. That means that she knows everything, knows that I'm her son, knows that I remember being lost in that airport. I couldn't speak. Not a single thought remained in my head. I didn't know how I should react: rejoice, take offense, fall apart.

"I'm so sorry, I thought you wouldn't understand." She was almost crying, but I didn't want to believe her tears.

"What was I wearing?"

"Excuse me?"

"What clothes was I wearing? You must have put a notice in the papers with a description. If you did, then you should be able to say what I was wearing."

"You were… my God, it's not that important. Do you want to ask me about something else? Like how I found you? How I've been all this time? Or who your father is or where we all used to live before you were abducted?"

"No one abducted me. I want to know what I was wearing. What was it? Answer me!"

"I… you were wearing… a red hoodie. A bit too big for you, probably a year left in it. Brand-new jeans – we'd just bought them – and brown boots. That's what you were wearing."

"What else?"

"That's everything you had on when I left you. I can remember turning back to look at you. You were sitting in the chair swinging your feet and looking at the people quietly, you didn't even cry."

"You looked back?"

No, she never looked back. There was also a gray cap and a kangaroo backpack. She ought to have remembered that.

And I almost believed her. What an idiot!

"You're not really my mother, are you?"

"What?"

"You're not telling the truth."

"You don't believe me? Who else knows as much about you as I do?"

"Where did you find out about this? Why would you suddenly decide to say you're my mother? Enough with the lying!" I'd lost the ability to stay calm and hadn't noticed that I'd jumped up from the sofa. What would you do in my place? I've been taken in like a fool, made fun of. "Who told you this story?"

She said nothing.

"Who?"

"You did…" she said.

"What?" My legs couldn't support me, and I sat back down.

"You told me the first day we met! I was showing you the apartment, and you were talking about something or other. Then you started telling me about how you'd been lost in an airport as a child. You said it all so freely, like it was nothing, to me, a stranger, and I was quite surprised. It's not everyone who would talk about something like that. But it never occurred to me to say I was your mother. That just happened now, out of the blue. I thought that you really wanted your real mother, and I really wanted to have a son. I never had any children… or a husband. I'm ashamed to admit that. I thought you could start visiting me, and we could sit and have tea… and… well, I don't know…"

Well, how do you like that? It's crazy. If I told my parents or wife about this, they'd send me straight to the nuthouse. I stood up and went to the door. Ever since I was a child I couldn't stand lies.

She stopped me at the threshold: "Wait."

"What else do you want? Maybe you can tell me you're my grandfather? The real one? And not the one who I spent summers with in the country? Or maybe you're that one, too – whatever. I'll believe whatever you say."

"No. I'm sorry. I really am very sorry."

Afterwards my parents told me that she was in a psychiatric hospital. And that she'd already been unwell... That explained a lot, but didn't make me feel any better. I felt sorry for myself: I'd almost found my mother, and despite the shock, confusion, and dissatisfaction at how things turned out, I felt a joy that I had never felt before in my life... But I felt much sorrier for her. What brought her to such madness? What could make someone pretend to be someone else's parent? Ordinary loneliness. That's all. I shuddered. I just realized that the same thing might happen to me.

7

I loved my fake parents just like any kid loves his real parents. They gave me a lot: not only what I needed, and not only what I wanted. That is, they gave me too much. They overdid it, basically. They wanted to turn me into a stable social unit like them, without wondering whether I wanted to be like them or a stable social unit. No matter how much I explained, they never understood – they still didn't – that I was not like that. My parents raised me as they thought they should, but they never bothered to ask whether that was what I needed. I certainly didn't live up to their expectations. Surely they never expected that the product of their efforts would be a thirty-year-old divorcé with no children, no prospects, no decent job, no savings and no place to call his own. I don't think they raised me to be a complete loser.

We didn't see each other much anymore. I moved around a lot. Rented apartments, other people's furniture, doors without spare keys – that's how I lived. The latest apartment, the one I was now locked out of, was also rented, three years already. I can't remember if my parents had visited since the move: they didn't come by that often. I'm not sure why: maybe because I disappointed them, or because they were just tired of me.

I got into a minibus. There were plenty of empty seats. I took a window seat, as had everyone else. Everyone was sitting on their own. I had noticed this a long time ago. When there are plenty of free seats, people always sit on their own. Even when there's a free seat next to someone, they'll take an uncomfortable seat just so they don't have to sit by someone else. Very few passengers at this time, it being pretty late. The peak hours had passed, and now the minibuses were transporting their night students, indistinguishable faces with indistinguishable occupations, and workaholics who were coming home late.

They all looked weird somehow, as if their faces were made of wax, staring glassily and frowning. God forbid you'd smile at someone. In the dark reflection of the minibus window I saw my own indistinct face. I was the same as them. But not quite: I felt a compulsion to smile, if only to prove that I was completely different. No, that's not it – it was to show that I used to be like them but didn't want to be anymore. I wanted to smile just for the sake of it and so other people would smile back at me. But was it worth it? Of course, I didn't smile in the end.

When I got off at the next to last stop, two other passengers got off with me. The minibus was empty, but nonetheless it continued along its scheduled route because that is what they do. I find this unbearably sad: the empty minibus keeps going to where it has no desire to go. And it will turn around at the last stop and start all over again. Perhaps no one will be there, and it will set off in the vain hope that someone still needs to go somewhere. Or it will wait at the last stop for two or three frozen strangers who will climb inside and sit on their own, with waxen faces, furrowed brows, and glassed-over faces without a hint of a smile.

My parents weren't home.

I sat down on a cold step in the stairwell, pulled out the pack of cigarettes, and lit one. This was the second time today I was sitting in front of a locked door. The orange-black flame flared in the darkness, but the smoke was not visible. The elevator started up. I listened: it rose to an upper floor and stopped. Not them.

That's how it goes! In a single evening I'd managed to be in two empty stairwells without keys in my pocket and feeling sorry for myself. I was thirty years old and I hadn't become anyone. Actually, I'd become a nobody. Not enough for a novel, certainly not enough to be a main character.

I spent a long time smoking. As long as is possible to smoke a single cigarette, until that orange-black flame nearly reached the filter. I stubbed it out, stood up from the cold steps and rang the bell again, just in case. No one opened the door. The elevator started again. It might have been them, but I wasn't going to wait and see, so I took the stairs.

8

It had become completely dark outside and much colder. The busses were still running, but since I had nowhere to go I set off on foot. I walked to the center of town, to the square in front of the Epiphany Church. I stood there awhile and went toward the embankment. Foolish teenagers were hanging out along the river, drunk, taking swigs out of the same bottle of beer, smoking and swearing loudly. They probably think this is what it's like to be all grown up. Funny.

I noticed this guy sitting in the stands at the stadium, where students are usually running laps in the morning, and where in the evening young people sit on benches drinking beer, warming themselves in the last rays of the setting sun, and everything about them shows that there's nowhere else they need to be right now. All of this is when it's warm; when it's cold, the place is deserted. So it was strange seeing this man here. He was dressed as if he was going to a party but forgot where he was going on the way. If he hadn't been in a suit and tie, I would have sped up and tried to get past without responding to his *have-you-got-a-cigarette?*

"I think so," I said. I walked up to him and sat down.

In the dim artificial light he seemed lost, like a boy, like I was once, though there was a difference of about forty years between that little boy and this man. But we were, all the same, quite similar.

"Aren't you cold without a coat?"

"No," he answered. The flame from the lighter sparked into the air and for a moment it seemed that all the lights went out.

"It's been a stupid day," I said, not because I didn't know what to say but because I really needed to share this stupid day with someone. "I locked myself out of my apartment."

The man looked at me:

"Yes, definitely a… stupid day. Your front door, was it? It happens. My daughter went and got married today. That also happens."

"Congratulations!" I said. "But why aren't you at the wedding?"

"It's over. The kids went home, and I thought I'd go for a walk and ended up here. You want some cognac?

"Wouldn't say no to that."

"That's great. Drink and you'll never be alone." He handed me the open bottle of cognac.

I took a sip and shuddered. Without food, the cognac tasted very strong.

He asked me for another cigarette.

"You know what, my daughter," he said, "I didn't want her when I found out my wife was pregnant. I was only twenty-two, and I thought I was too young to have kids. I didn't know if I wanted kids at all, but now... I know that the one good thing in my life, the only thing I don't regret, is my daughter... All my life I've been afraid of making a mistake, but all I've ever done is make mistakes."

"Same here," I said, the words accompanied by a thin white vapor. "But today I realized that it might not be too late to change. I quit my job."

"Really? You quit?"

"Yes. I wrote a letter of resignation and walked out. Just like that, just like I've always wanted to."

"Now you're going to stop doing what you hate and start doing what you want, am I right?"

"Yes. Except that I'm not entirely sure what I want to do."

He laughed: "No problem, friend, you'll figure it out. I wonder if I could do something like that. No, it's much too late for me. You're still young. What line of work were you in? Why'd you leave?"

"I didn't have a particularly interesting job." For some reason I was ashamed to tell him what I did for a living; and I was ashamed to admit to myself that I had squandered a large portion of my life.

"Well, it couldn't be any worse than what I do." He burst out laughing. "Want to know where I work? The customer hotline for Old Spice. You know the commercial where the guy is running in the mountains without sweating, and then someone says, 'you can see for yourself, and if you think you can prove us wrong, give us a call and we'll give you a full refund' – or something like that, more or less. Well, I'm the guy who answers those calls! I'm not joking! Could you imagine a more useless or pathetic job than that?"

He let out a hysterical, nervous, and empty laugh. While I waited for him to collect himself, I had more cognac and thought about the strange things that had happened today. None of it was stranger than finally meeting someone with the same job as me. I'd thought there wasn't anyone like me. But there he was! Sitting right here, not at all like I imagined him. And I liked him. I didn't tell him about my job – there was no chance he'd have believed me.

Once he finished laughing, we lit fresh cigarettes and sat quietly for some time. My fingers were frozen, but apart from that everything was fine, and I didn't feel the cold.

I told him everything.

"When I was five, me and my mom were going to fly somewhere, or maybe getting back from somewhere, but anyway we were at the airport. She put me in a chair and said that I should wait for her and that she'd be back in a minute. But she never came back."

He looked at me:

"Really?"

"Yes. I know it's hard to believe, but there you go."

"What happened after that?"

"Nothing much. I was found by a man and woman who became my new parents."

"Hmm. So did you ever find your real mother?"

"I haven't looked."

"Why not?"

"I didn't want to, so I never tried. My wife – my ex-wife – says that I made it all up, but she doesn't know, she doesn't know what I know, and it's easier for her to say I made it up than to admit that it might be the truth."

He was quiet. He lit another cigarette. Maybe he didn't believe me either. Maybe you too don't really believe me, maybe you also think that I imagined it all, that such things just don't happen, that no one can lose their child in an airport. But in fact every kind of thing can happen in this life, and if it's hard for us to believe something, then maybe that has more to do with ourselves than with whether this "something" is real or not. Well? What do you think?

Finally he said:

"We all lose someone, and sometimes get lost too."

"Like keys…"

"Yes, like keys. And someone will find them eventually."

"Lost keys, a lost person, a thing lost, in due time everything will find its place."

I took another sip of cognac; it seemed we understood one another very well.

We talked late into the night. Talked until the trams found their way back to the depot, until the last revelers got home, until newlyweds went to sleep, until the last drop of cognac was drunk and the last cigarette smoked, until we were so cold our teeth chattered, until it had come time for us to go back home.

We talked about everything; we weren't afraid of admitting that we'd been unlucky in life and that we were lonely despite being surrounded by people. We talked in the way that only strangers can talk, with the knowledge that we would never see one another again, so we didn't have to lie, because there was no reason to; we didn't have to worry about what the other thought of us, because we didn't give a damn what he thought.

9

Finally I understood why, after ending up on that empty landing, I had begun this purposeless wandering around the city, trying to find my place in the world; and I remembered why I had been thinking so long and hard about my real mother: what I really wanted would never come true, because what I wanted was impossible.

What I wanted was to be a five-year-old again sitting in the airport, kicking my feet because they don't quite reach the floor and I could kick as much as I liked. I wanted my mother to return and say: "Sorry I was so long. Did you get bored?" I wanted her to hug me tight and say: "I was so worried that I might never see you again."

So that was my unrealizable desire… I was thirty years old, and my feet always reached the floor. I couldn't swing them back and forth, and no matter how long I sat in the airport, my mother would never return and say: "Sorry I was so long. Did you get bored?"

But then: So what? Thinking about that made me waste thirty years of my life, and I couldn't let it ruin the next thirty, or more if I'm lucky. These thoughts made a chill run down my spine, and I was shivering.

And all of a sudden it began to snow. It really did, I'm not making it up. The first snow of the year, which for some reason was going not downward but upward. I smiled. My God, I couldn't remember the last time I smiled… it was like I was five again, with my whole life still ahead of me. I laughed joyfully. And why not? No one could hear me, and even if someone could, I wouldn't have cared: I wanted to laugh and rejoice while I could, while I felt happy

She lost me in an airport. I'd been sitting there to this very day, in that same chair. Sitting and waiting for something to happen at any moment, not understanding that things kept happening. Perhaps you don't need anything major? Perhaps all you need is to lock yourself out, sit down on an empty landing, and start searching for some meaning in your life? And to find out that it's not really that bad?

Mistakes, failures, unhappiness – what of it? If you don't know the meaning of sadness, melancholy, and despair, then you will never know the meaning of happiness. People treasure true happiness because they know how fleeting it is. They have a keen sense for it and gather up every sliver of that happiness wherever it may be found. In the smile of the girl from next door, in bright yellow autumn leaves, in the dance of a flame, in a friend's joke, in love, whether it be returned or not, and in hatred, in cold steps, in a lonely airport departure hall.

Tomorrow I would figure out something and go back home. I told you that it didn't mean much to me, but that's not true, it was all a lie. I loved my apartment. I loved everything about it! I loved the ashtray a colleague brought back from Egypt, which was chipped long ago. I loved my Bart Simpson mug, which I used for coffee in the morning and tea in the evening. I loved my fifteen-channel TV. I loved the green mat by the door and the photograph held up with magnets on the refrigerator, the one of me and Gennady at some party a few years ago, still young and so ridiculous: I've got my arm around his shoulders, he's making a face, and we're laughing. I loved these things, which were all dear to me no matter what. I was ready to go home…

I wandered the town for a long time, down side streets and through squares, and then sat at the Strelka and looked out at the water. Music reached me from somewhere, a cold wind was blowing, and I drifted off to sleep on a bench on the embankment, laying my head on my arms, wrapped up in my coat. I was deliriously happy.

Translated by Christopher Tauchen

Eight Days
until the Dawn

EIGHT DAYS UNTIL THE DAWN

1

This happened in 1998. Or was it '99? I can't remember now. Anyway, it was one of those years, doesn't matter which. Time seems to get stuck sometimes, so that you can't tell whether it exists at all. One day follows another, month follows month, and there's never a break in the sequence: November comes after October, May goes before June. One year, two, three – from a distance, each one seems fuzzy and indistinguishable, like mice scurrying in a cellar. All that remains are our recollections: the memory preserves them, leaving only feelings, smells, colors. Sometimes there's a flash in the mind: a song lyric, the name of a film or once-famous actor, titles of books, advertising slogans. And only then can we be certain that those events actually took place.

You can begin any story like that, with a date. Like dates have any meaning. Maybe they do in history books, but they don't for me. My own dates and history have been removed from my memory, as if someone went over them with an eraser. For me, those days are marked not by red numbers on a calendar but by an open road leading south, by the smell of asphalt melting slowly in the sun. Sometimes in summer or late spring I'm struck by this smell and my head swims in reverie. I find that I'm no longer on my way home or to work but in another dimension, and I can clearly see our old car, greyish-white, with a scratch on the rear passenger door. Not some fancy foreign make, but one of "ours", an ordinary Lada hatchback.

Picture this: I'm sitting there with my arm hanging out the window, and from time to time, only for a second, I stick out my head, and the wind blows and plays with my hair, which gets into my mouth and eyes so that I can't see a thing. It's quite warm for the beginning of summer, but the wind carries off the heat before I can really feel it. Everything is good. I take off my sandals and tuck my feet in underneath me. I wish I could stick my feet out the window as well.

I'm watching him on the sly, observing how he drives. He's so goofy. But then, he's always been like that, always a bit ridiculous. And in the car this natural ridiculousness is all the more obvious. He's like a little boy who's taken his dad's jeep without asking: now that he's at the wheel, he doesn't know what to do with it. He's looking at me, too, and smiling.

"Are you laughing at me?" he said. "Just you wait, soon you'll be the one driving, and it'll be my turn to make fun."

I laugh and say nothing.

That was our first day on the road. As I continue from here, I might get the order of things mixed up and confuse certain events and conversations, but I know that first day is fixed perfectly in my mind, every minute detail and feeling. I remember the last day less well, perhaps, but then I passed through it as if through a fog. But the first day was a real gift. I'd give anything for another day like that.

We left early in the morning when everyone was still asleep. Not only our small town and our parents were still asleep, but also the road itself. The sun had just begun to wake up. Somewhere in the east it was stretching itself out and smiling at us, the first travelers of the day.

We're driving into the wind, joyful and happy, and it

feels like it will be like this forever. If we keep going like this, forgetting about everything in the world, renouncing our past lives, not thinking about the future, then everything will always be okay.

He starts singing: *There is nothing better in this world...* He's imitating someone's voice, but I can't work out whose. I'm laughing out of sheer happiness, just because the song came to him.

I pick it up: *Then for friends to up and hit the road...*

And him again: *To them no route is ever uninspiring...*

And then we both fall silent.

"Um... what's the next part?" he asks.

"I was hoping you'd know."

"I do... it's on the tip of my tongue."

"I think there's something about an alarm."

"Yeah, something like: *We're not scared of... da dada... alaa-arms*. No, that's not it."

"I can't remember it at all."

We agonized for another half-hour trying to remember the rest of the song from "The Bremen Musicians", but in the end we decided just to sing the first three lines.

There is nothing better in this world
Then for friends to up and hit the road
To them no route is ever uninspiring
....

We had a lot in common, which is probably why we got to be such good friends. Neither of us stood out among our peers: we weren't good-looking, rich, or cool. No one noticed us, and we had no friends. These similarities are what brought us together. Had one of us been distinguishable is some way or had lots of friends there's no way we'd have even spoken to one another. Nobody talks to people like us.

I didn't go to school that day. It's not like I did this often, and I wasn't a particularly bad student. There just wasn't anything for me to do there. I hated it: school, the teachers, my classmates. All of it made me sick. I hated them because they hated me, though I'm still not sure why they did. I suppose everyone needs to have somebody to hate, or at least to feel superior to.

I did try to make friends with the other girls at school, just because it's done. None of them were ever openly rude: if I asked a question they would answer politely, if unenthusiastically, but they never let me copy off them or borrow money, nothing like that. They would gather in little packs to talk about some poor devil from another class, or flick through idiotic teen magazines under their desks. They never let me into their group, and I never tried to force my way in. I understood that I was an outcast in my own school, and that there was nothing I could do about it.

I took a seat on a bench overlooking the soccer field. The P.E. classes were inside that day – too cold and wet outside – so I wasn't worried about getting caught. I looked at the gray sky and watched the harried, lonely commuters shortening their journeys by cutting through the school grounds. That's when I first saw him. He walked right up to me: he was scrawny and not very good-looking. Not at all the type that teenage girls tend to fall in love with.

"Got a smoke?" he asked.

I handed him an open pack.

"What school do you go to? No. 8?"

"Uh huh."

"Why aren't you in class?"

"What's it to you?" I said. "Where are you supposed to be, the lycée?"

"Yep."

The lycée was just across from my school and was thought to be one of the better places to get an education. The kids who went there came from rich families that could afford the substantial monthly payments. Some – the rare exceptions – were scholarship kids who had earned good grades and passed the entrance exam. I'd heard that they made up only about ten percent of the student body, so the vast majority of the students were rich kids, all of them handsome, well-groomed, impeccably dressed, and cheerful. I knew absolutely nothing about the world they belonged to, and I didn't want to learn.

"Oh," I said, disappointed. "So you're one of them."

"One of who?"

"One of those rich kids."

"You assume I'm rich just because I go there?"

I shrugged.

"Well, you're wrong," he said.

"Then how'd you end up there?"

"I'm just too damn smart." He said this with such a serious look on his face that I couldn't help but laugh. He smiled bashfully, pleased to have been able to cheer me up.

We sat on the bench and talked for a while. It was nice. Or maybe it just seemed nice because it was the first time I had ever been taken for a real human being instead of just a silent, senseless presence. It turns out that talking to someone else can be quite interesting. When you only talk to yourself, you can discuss whatever you want, you always agree, and you always seem to be the most intelligent and interesting person. But now it turned out that there was something even more interesting: other people.

Next he made it clear that he was just like me. He didn't say this in so many words, but I understood it, I knew what he was about. He wasn't well liked at his school, probably even less so than me. He wasn't like them: not rich, not good-looking, not popular. He got good grades, and the teachers always held him up as an example to the other students. This annoyed his classmates more than anything else, and they barely spoke to him. He was the outcast in his world, just like I was in mine.

"So, where are we stopping today?" he asks.

"Don't know yet."

"Would you take a look at the map?"

"It's a bit early for that."

"Come on, I'm starving," he said. "Let's stop somewhere."

We stop for lunch at the first roadside café we come across. Later we would encounter a lot of these places, and they all looked the same, like in that kid's game where you have to spot the difference. But this first one I remember best of all, probably because it was the first. Out in front there are umbrellas and sticky white plastic tables that haven't been cleaned for a long time. It's not any better inside. We place an order at the counter and say we'll wait for it outside.

"It's a bit chilly," the waitress says. We shrug it off, no big deal.

She, this girl, is somehow lifeless. Wayward strands stick out from her long unwashed hair, and her eyes are sad, like autumn. Like when the last yellowed leaves have fallen, and an uneasy winter will arrive any day: dull and dreary. That's about how her eyes were.

There is no one else at the café, inside or out. We'd ordered some salad and kebabs. While we're waiting for the kebabs we can smell the fire and the roasting meat from behind the café. It's not cold outside, but there is a lot of dust and wind. The waitress brings our kebabs on plastic plates. Each plate has five pieces of meat and a pile of marinated onion. I think then that I've never had such delicious meat. We're as delighted as we'd be if we were eating in a fancy restaurant. We both laugh, and I notice the girl watching us through the dirty window at the counter. I feel sorry for her. I can tell she's an outcast, too. She's one of us.

In the car the music is blaring and we're picking up speed. We're racing down the highway and singing along to Bon Jovi's "It's My Life". We sing song after song until we've had enough. For dinner we break into our supplies: cookies, apples, candy, a bottle of mineral water. We count the oncoming cars while we're eating, transforming this into a fun game.

I can't remember the name of the town where we stayed that first night: we passed through so many of them on our trip. I know I'd only need to glance at the map to remember it – the place is marked in red pencil – but I want to keep its name a secret even from myself. When I can't remember something from that time, I think it means it wasn't actually that important, and that's how it ought to remain.

We took a room in a small hotel and went up to the second floor. It was a small hotel by the highway, not dirty, but not particularly spotless either. A run-of-the-mill hotel, the sort frequented by long-haul truck drivers.

We'd cleaned ourselves up and were now lying in bed.

"Are you asleep?" I ask. It's a double bed, but that doesn't bother us: we're just friends, after all. There's nothing wrong with friends sleeping in the same bed.

"Nope."

"What's wrong?"

"Nothing. Just can't sleep."

"Do you think it was a good idea for us to leave?"

"I don't know."

"I think it was."

We lay there in the same bed in some small hotel in some small town. We are somewhere in the middle of nowhere. We don't know the town or the people who live here, and the people don't know us, which means that, in a way, we don't exist. As I fall asleep I wonder: What if I wake up tomorrow and none of this has happened? What if I'm not in this chilly hotel room with my friend by my side? If they've been replaced by my own familiar bed, posters on the wall, and the smell of breakfast cooking in the kitchen. I find his warm hand next to me and squeeze it hard. I want to make sure that these feelings of happiness and freedom are real, that they won't disappear when I open my eyes.

2

That morning I didn't feel like going to school, so I decided: *I'm not going, and that's that!* The day before I'd happened to overhear some of the other girls talking about me in the school bathroom. They said I wasn't normal, that I had something wrong with my head. Apparently I was in a cult. It was pretty much all nonsense. And that's not counting the fact that I'm a fat ugly cow. It's not like people said nice things about me before, and I wasn't that upset at the time, but all the same it left a bitter taste in my mouth. I brushed my teeth about five times that evening, but that still didn't make it go away.

The next day I left at exactly eight o'clock and rushed off to school. But after two blocks I slowed down and started in a completely different direction. It was the end of autumn: a fierce wind was blowing, and there was a fine rain. My sneakers were soaked instantly, and my teeth started chattering from the cold. I'm not sure how, but I suddenly discovered that I was standing in front of his apartment building. I went in, climbed the stairs, and sat on a step between the fifth and sixth floors. I didn't have to wait long: he came out after ten minutes or so. He didn't notice me at first. He spent a long time fiddling with his keys in the door, singing to himself:

Supergirl... and supergirlsdon't cry... my supergirl...

But suddenly he looked up, saw me, and then – as if nothing had happened – said:

"So I guess we're not going to school today."

In his kitchen we drank tea from blue teacups and ate chocolates. I put my shoes and socks on the radiator to dry. I can still remember these small details: the pattern on the cups, the brand of the chocolates, my two bare feet. Sometimes I have a hard time remembering what I had for dinner last night, but I've never forgotten that small bowl of chocolates, those famous Bears of the North.

We sat there quietly smoking my cigarettes. I felt like we were pretending to be other people. We weren't ourselves, but characters in a soap opera. I played at being the aloof teenage girl, and he was the affable heartthrob who always had a shoulder to cry on. I was trying to hold my cigarette in such a way that I looked pretty from the side. But we weren't on television, and we had to remember to open a window so the smell would be gone before his mother came back for lunch.

Our affectations disappeared when we went into his room. We became ourselves again, teenagers who were skipping school. And we never went back to pretending.

His room was a complete mess. He had stuff strewn everywhere: CDs, cassettes, books, papers. The walls were covered over with pages torn from music magazines: there were foreign bands – Red Hot Chili Peppers, John Bon Jovi, Marilyn Manson, Guano Apes, Radiohead, No Doubt – and some that were closer to home – OkeanElzy, VopliVidopliassova, Zemfira, Mumiy Troll. Somehow a poster for The X-Files had made it into the mix.

I'd just begun to take a look at the cassettes lying beside the old stereo when he asked me what I listened to.

"The radio," I said.

"What do you mean, *the radio*?" He was so serious-looking, his mouth half open in surprise. I can remember thinking then: how sweet and funny he is.

Later on he would get me up to speed on all the music he listened to, even gave me many of his CDs and cassettes.

We'd spend forever choosing CDs, hours hanging out in music stores.

"How do you know so much about music?" I asked him that day.

"Take a look," he said, tossing me a few issues of *NME* magazine, which I'd never seen before.

"My brother gets them for me in Moscow," he said after seeing my confusion. "You can't find anything here, even when it's supposedly in stock. Apparently there's piles of this stuff in Moscow. He says I've got to keep up with the times."

"You have a brother?" I said. "I thought you were an only child."

"Well, he's not exactly my brother." he said. "More like my mom's bother – my uncle – but I still call him my brother."

"What's he doing in Moscow? Working?"

"Something like that. He sells cars, sometimes fixes them up or sells them for parts. I'm not sure exactly, haven't really asked. He's our only relative. Except for my dad and my grandmother, of course, but he left us a long time ago. The two of them live here." He pointed to a place on the map on the wall.

"That's pretty far away."

We could never have imagined then that we would soon be on our way to that very same place on the map.

3

"I told you to check the map and see how much farther we have, and you just said 'We've got time, we'll make it.' It's getting dark now and we've still got to find a hotel."

"Would you calm down? I'm the one who's driving. Why don't you try to get some sleep?"

"Seriously? Why didn't you look at the map?"

"Just shut up, would you?" I looked at him out of the corner of my eye, and we both burst out laughing.

The day was coming to a close. It had rained recently on the road, and the air was clean and fresh. The newly painted dividing line glowed brightly under the dim streetlamps. For a long time he said nothing while he watched the night thicken outside the window, and then he said:

"Guess what I was just thinking about."

"I have no idea."

"Our dance. Do you remember?"

"Of course I do! How could I forget that?"

If it hadn't been for my best friend, there's no way I'd have gone to my graduation ball. People think that that night is probably the most important event in your time at school, but for me it was a symbol of the end of my former life and the beginning of a new one, sort of like New Year's, when you can promise yourself over and again that you'll stop being like you used to be.

"I couldn't survive it there without you," I told him at the time. And he understood. He always understood everything.

So many of my classmates had been transformed that night: they were wearing long evening gowns, short skirts and blouses from the most expensive stores. The boys, identical in their suits, were checking the girls out from head to toe. At the time I thought that I had chosen the perfect outfit: a long dark-blue pleated skirt with large blood-red flowers, a good Gipsy-style imitation, and a matching red top with three-quarter-length sleeves. I was wearing large hoop earrings and had somehow managed to force my stubborn curly hair into a chignon. As for my makeup, I followed all the rules in the magazines, and when I looked in the mirror I found a stranger. For a moment I even thought this stranger was almost beautiful!

All my efforts turned to dust when it came time to receive my diploma. I wasn't used to walking in heels, but all the same

I'd gone and bought them. Terribly expensive, but gorgeous: black, with thin straps and an open heel. As I was walking up the stairs, I got tangled in the folds of my Gipsy skirt, lost my balance, and tripped. I very nearly fell to the ground, but at the last instant managed to catch the railing. Laughter spread through the hall, audible in patches here and there. I felt an unruly lock of hair fall out of place and hang lifelessly in front of my face. Panicked, not knowing where to look, I saw my friend. He was standing to the side of the stage with the crowd of relatives and other people who weren't supposed to be there. He was smiling at me admiringly and sincerely, as if this embarrassment of mine had never happened, or maybe as if he hadn't noticed. Perhaps he hadn't. That alone is what kept me from turning around. I smiled back at him and continued walking toward the podium.

The party afterwards was boring and depressing. I watched the other students taking part in games and dancing. I remembered my disgrace, and at the time it seemed that nothing more awful could ever happen to me. I was so stupid, so ridiculous! My friend was with me, of course, but even he couldn't cheer me up. We were both like foreign bodies and they had to put up with us, but now they acted as if we weren't even there.

"I'll be back in a minute," I said as I got up from my seat.

My classmate Sveta Volkova was standing by the bathrooms with a boy from another class. They were kissing and pressing close to one another. He had his hands under her blouse, and she was unbuttoning his shirt. Volkova opened her eyes and saw me looking at her. She smiled at me. Then, without any malice or mockery in her tone, she said:

"What are you staring at?" Do you want some of this? Why don't you stop drooling over us and go hang out with your freak of a boyfriend."

The boy laughed and, without a moment's glance toward

me, stuck his tongue back into Volkova's mouth. I walked past them with my head down. My cheeks were burning.

In the bathroom I sat down on a closed toilet seat and buried my face in my hands. My hands were trembling as I got the cigarettes from my bag and lit one. I took out a small bottle with a cocktail of vodka and cranberry juice. We'd stocked up on these before the ceremony. I took small sips from the bottle and winced. My head started to spin a little, and a pleasant wave made its way through my body. For several minutes I sat there collecting myself. And suddenly I realized: I'm done with school now. This will be the last time I walk through its corridors. I'm not going to miss it. And it won't miss me either.

I let down my hair and splashed some water on my face. My cheeks burned like fire, and I heaved a sigh of relief. I went back to the assembly hall with my head raised proudly. No one paid any attention to me, but then I wasn't there for anyone else's sake – I was there for myself and my own sense of pride. My pride was the only one to see me, cheering me on from the side. On that day even this approval was enough for me.

"Let's get out of here," I said to my friend, and without a word he got up and followed me out.

We wandered around the city late into the night. I was stumbling in my stupid heels, hating them with all my heart. We drank, we smoked, we sat on benches, and we watched the sunrise.

"Didn't you want to dance the waltz?" he asked.

Of course I did! But the waltz was for the most beautiful girls in the school, who danced, as you'd expect, with the most handsome boys. No one even asked me. It didn't even occur to anyone that I might want them to.

"Yes," I said, having thought all this. "I did."

"In that case, may I have this dance?" He rose and gave me his hand.

"Yeah, right."

"I'm serious! Stand up!"

And we started to dance: no music, no spectators, no evening gowns.

"One-two-three," he chanted, "one-two-three, one-two-three."

We were not good dancers – we shifted around awkwardly, repeating our steps with an unfathomable persistence. The rising sun shone on us, as a stage light might snatch something interesting from the darkness, and somewhere in the depths of our consciousness music began to sound, and it seemed that we were dancing perfectly and that now, at this exact moment, the world was bearing witness to the most beautiful dance that had ever been.

At his graduation ball we sat at a table and drank beer. Someone had brought a whole case, and we helped ourselves. Then my friend showed me the girl he'd been in love with for the last two years. His Angela was beautiful, very beautiful indeed.

"I don't like her," I lied. "She's nothing special."

But when a slow dance started, I told him he ought to ask her.

"She wouldn't say yes," he said as he was fiddling with the tablecloth.

I knew this, but for some reason I wanted him to be completely aware of it, I wanted him to feel more rejected than he'd ever been. I was horrified by these thoughts and turned away so I wouldn't have to look him in the eyes.

That night I kept an eye on my friend, who never took his own eyes off Angela. In his white shirt and new pressed trousers he looked even more ridiculous than usual. I felt such pity for him and for myself: I knew just how much he wanted to look good that day, that he had gotten all dressed up in the secret hope that he would suddenly become more handsome and that, for this one night, he would somehow be popular. I knew this because it was the same for me. At those two graduations we saw ourselves for what we really were. We learned that ugly ducklings stay ugly, and that swans give birth to swans, and that the swans swim separately from the ducklings and never go near them if they can help it. We learned that fairy tales exist somewhere outside reality.

We stop at a gas station just in time: we've nearly run out. While the gas is pumping he examines the car from head to tail. I take a look at the map.

"We're going to be driving all night…"

"Really? That's great!" he says.

"What's great about that?"

"I don't know. I like driving at night."

"Are you on a road trip?" asks the gas station attendant. He's young, maybe twenty-five, and has a mangy dog constantly at his feet.

"Yes," my friend says, and he names the city we're going to.

"Wow," he says, surprised. "That's a long way from here! The roads are more dangerous at night."

"There aren't as many cars at night," I say.

"What if you come across the ghost car? Aren't you afraid?" He laughs, but I start to feel uneasy.

"Oh, so there's one of them around here?" says my friend.

"Of course!" the attendant says, chuckling. "There's the ghost of a Mercedes wandering these parts, sort of like the Flying Dutchman. So be careful. You may just happen to meet him."

We drive off, and I think about how we meet different people every day on our trip. We don't see them for more than ten minutes, but their particular characteristics, like the expression in their eyes, their smiles, their words, stick in my mind. It's not the same with people we've known since childhood. Their images fade and grow dim, while we will always remember these brief acquaintances as if they're our own family. There are a lot of these people: waitresses, bartenders, gas station attendants, hotel porters. Ordinary people living ordinary lives. There's nothing special about them, but we still remember them.

Toward nightfall my friend falls asleep, and I drive the car through the silence and the onrushing darkness. We're driving along this sleeping highway completely on our own. I speed up a bit but then slow down. I can barely see the road, and you never know who you might encounter: a squirrel or a deer, or God knows what else. I think about the ghost of the old Mercedes that the attendant told us about. Of course I know he was joking, but I'm seized by small waves of terror. If it weren't for my friend sleeping so peacefully next to me, the panic would surely overcome me, and I'd go as fast as I could to the nearest town which was still so very far away. But his face, so calm, so childlike, so peaceful, has calmed my fear, and I can relax and smile.

4

On the fourth day we make a stop at the next town. We need a break from our long journey and want to explore some of the unfamiliar streets and bars. We check in at a small hotel by the river port. The room overlooks the river, but because the window doesn't open all we can see is the grimy smudges on the glass.

The road has made us too tired to go out for a walk, but the room is too stuffy and unpleasant to stay in. The manager suggests that we go to a club not too far from here, so we set off in that direction.

It's drizzling; the nightclub's sign – which promises us a "great time" – is a flash of bright neon. Taxis come and go, and I see people inside drinking champagne. The bouncers pay us no attention, as if this were in the usual order of things.

Dance music of some kind is blaring, and we sit down at an empty table only to be run off by a waitress who informs us that all the tables are reserved. We ask if anyone has reserved the stools at the bar, and she says rudely: "Apparently not."

We sit at the bar and observe the drunken crowd. Teenagers, made-up girls in miniskirts, boys in tracksuits. "What are we doing here?" I ask myself.

"A special drink for the young couple," says the bartender as he places two shot glasses in front of us and sets them alight. "Drink up, but do it fast, all in one go. You'll like it. It'll knock your head off."

"We're not a couple," says my friend.

"Really? That's odd."

What I find odd is that we're taken for a couple all of a sudden. And then, because we're not, I start to feel lonely. Sure, I like traveling with my best friend: I'm free as a bird, don't need anything more from life. Or do I? What if it wasn't him sitting next to me, but someone I was in love with? What then? Would I look at him with love-struck eyes, just as he looked at me, and would the bartender make us a "special drink for the young couple"?

As I'm thinking all this, my friend has met some long-legged girl who he is now slow-dancing with on the dance floor. Nothing like this would ever happen if we went to a club at home. But no one knows us here, and we don't know anyone else. We can be anyone we like, play whatever role we want.

Once we left our town – which never allowed us any role but those of outcast and loser – we discovered in ourselves the strength and the talent to play confident young people without a care in the world. As soon as that happened, all our self-doubt and fear went away. This is how he picked up that girl so fast. She's not a bad one either: long legs, blonde, and pretty as well. It's strange to think, but he doesn't seem as ridiculous standing next to her as he used to.

"Why the long face?" says the bartender.

I shrug.

"Jealous?"

"What? Of him?" I say, surprised.

"Sure."

"No way... we're just friends..."

"Well, you sure look like you're jealous."

It's 4 a.m. My friend has left, and I don't know where he's gone. I go outside to get some fresh air. I stand on the steps leading up to the club and lean on the railing.

"Hey," says a voice suddenly from behind me, "want to go for a walk? I heard that you're traveling. I can show you around." It's the bartender. "My shift is over, but the busses aren't running yet and I'm too lazy to walk home."

I shrug.

"Sure, why not?"

"It's cold. Here, take my jacket."

A strong breeze blows from the river where the water is dark and unsettled. We take a long set of steps to the upper level of the embankment where I can see both the river and the embankment itself stretching out into the distance. Waves are rocking the large boats at the quayside. Somewhere inside tourists are sleeping peacefully. I'm not the least bit sleepy. We are alone, it's all quiet and calm around as we walk along the embankment. On the right there is a row of 19th-century mansions which are mostly museums nowadays; to the left is the river. The bartender shows me the "Pavilion of Love." From a distance its columns look white, but as we get close I can see that the paint is peeling and that the columns are covered in phone numbers and confessions of love: "Dima P., I love you!" "Girls – want to meet up?" "Kirill + Lena = eternal love" "We were here March 6. Great place. Will come again!" "Misha is a cheating bastard!!!" "Vasya was here 23 April." And so on.

"Everyone thinks they've got to write something," says the bartender. "I did the same when I was a kid." He smiles. "Legend has it that some guy met his wife this way. They repaint it every spring, but someone always comes along and starts it all over again."

I wrap myself up in his jacket, and we take turns smoking a cigarette. We look out onto the river. It's already getting light outside.

I follow him wherever he leads. He takes me to the Strelka, a pointed bit of land where the city's two rivers meet. From that height we can see some fountains, which are turned off at this late hour, and beds of flowers that spell out the name of the town.

We sit on the rostrum of a large stadium and look at a church with pale walls and round scaled domes in verdant green. In the predawn silence the church seems peaceful and majestic. The bench beneath us is cold and wet with dew, and I fidget sitting on his jacket.

"When are you leaving town?" he asks.

"Don't know yet."

"There's a rock concert here tomorrow. You should come."

"I doubt we'll still be here."

He shrugs and reaches for a cigarette.

"Have you always lived here?" I ask him.

"Yes," he says. "Have you been traveling long?"

"Feels like it."

"I envy you. I'd love to go somewhere, but I probably won't ever get around to it."

"Why would you want to leave? It's so nice and beautiful here!"

He shrugs.

"It's all so ordinary to me. Every year it's the same – the same festivals in this stadium, the same amusements in the amusement park, the same beer stalls. Everyone knows everyone else, and you always know someone who knows someone else who knows you. You go out with your friends' old girlfriends. It's a vicious circle. An oversized village. Do you think all I want to do in life is work in that shitty club and watch hockey? But supposing I was to start a course in economics and graduate, I'd get a diploma, but then what? I'd trade the bar for an office, and nothing else would change."

"Do you think it would be better somewhere else?"

He shrugs a second time.

A runner wearing shorts and a shirt with the number seven comes into the stadium. He begins with some stretching, then runs laps around the track. We're curious and watch him run, but he pays us no attention, as if we weren't there at all.

He takes me back to the hotel, and I give him my number on a scrap of paper.

"If you ever find yourself nearby, give me a call," I say. "I'd love to see you again…"

"Thanks," he says. Then he turns his head strangely and tells me something that no one has ever said, something I've never even dreamed of hearing. He says it sincerely – I can see that – and there's no reason for him to lie. It's not like we're going to see one another again.

"You know what, you're really cool… I've never met a girl like you before. He's lucky to have you. Even if you are just friends…"

5

Things have never been this awkward between us. I'm driving in silence. Apart from a quick "good morning" we haven't said a thing to one another. He is smoking and flicking the ash out the window.

"When did you get back?" he says finally.

"Not sure exactly. It was light out."

"Where were you?"

"I could ask you the same question."

He doesn't respond, and we drive on in silence. Now he's driving, and I'm smoking.

I can't live without you – a song is playing on the radio. I tap my foot in time with the music, and in my head I'm singing along. It's playing at full volume. I prefer it like this: no worrying about what to say. This is one of our favorite songs, but today for some reason I find it annoying, and for the first time I really want to be home with my mother. I want to stop the car and turn back. And drive ridiculously fast so I can get home faster. Suddenly my head is spinning, a lump is rising in my throat, and I feel like I'm choking.

When I open my eyes, he's leaning over me, frightened…

"Hey, are you… are you okay?" he asks.

"I don't know. What was that?"

"I think you fainted. Drink this." He hands me a bottle of water. His eyes are wide with fear. I find this funny, but I don't have the strength to laugh.

"I'm sorry," he said.

"What for?"

"I was being an idiot. I was mad at you."

"What for?" I said again.

"I don't know. It really got to me that you were with that bartender…"

"But you were the one who left first, with that girl…"

We're eating lunch in the Black Cat Café, which we found eventually after a long search through the streets of this anonymous town. We're the only ones here. On the wall a buzzing TV set is playing a soccer match, but we sit with our backs to it. I'm not hungry, but he begs me to eat. Then he says I won't be driving. He is just as tired as I am, but he will be driving himself.

At the hotel he puts me to bed, even though I don't feel bad anymore. I'm glad to be lounging around under the covers: I eat everything he brings me from the nearby shop and listen to him talk.

"Nothing happened with her," he says all of a sudden. He just says it, I don't even have to ask.

"Same here."

"Why hasn't anything like this happened before? That someone suddenly thinks we're worth talking to?"

"That was at home. We're different here. More like we really are, not like everyone's used to seeing us."

6

"So you've never cried? Not at all?"

"Not really, not that I can remember."

"Not even when you saw *Titanic*?"

"Are you kidding? I fell asleep halfway through! I still don't know how it ended."

"But what about when you fell down or skinned you knees, or if you got a burn or smacked into something and it really hurt. Didn't you cry then?"

"Not really. How's crying going to help? You've just got to deal with the pain…"

"What about when you found out that people were laughing at you. Did you cry then?"

"No, that never bothered me. It never would've occurred to me to cry."

He thinks about that for a while.

"What about when we have to say goodbye, after we get there, and you're driving back through all these places we've been to together, except that you're alone... Won't you cry then? And when you get back home, when you visit our park... What about then?"

I think about what he just said: of course it's easier to say no, but I try to imagine it. Over the course of this past year when, after finishing school, we pretended to be students at the engineering college when in fact we never went anywhere, just spent all day hanging out together, and I spent more time with him than with myself – he became a part of me. How can you say goodbye to part of yourself?

"I don't know..." I say.

Now I really don't know.

We say nothing. We're both probably trying to imagine what's going to happen, but nothing about our future is clear.

"So you've never really been in love?" he asks.

We've drawn the curtains in our room and are sitting on the floor drinking and eating olives and sandwiches with smoked sausage. I'm leaning against the bedside table, and he's got his back against the bed. Between us is an ashtray piled high with cigarette butts. We're well into our second hour of this and have had quite a lot to drink.

"And I suppose you have?" I ask. "You can spare me all that talk about your Angela. What a stupid name. That's not love... I can't believe you're really in love with this doll. All she's got is a nice ass."

He grins.

"Maybe it wasn't love, though she really does have a nice ass... All the same, I can at least name a person I have some feelings for. Can you do that?

"Thom Yorke."

"I'm serious."

"Me too."

We're quiet for a while, then I start talking excitedly, trying to fit in everything I have to say before I change my mind.

"What's the point?" I say. "Take a look at me – sure, I'm your friend and you won't say anything bad about my looks, but I'm a realist and I can see my reflection in the mirror. What good is falling in love when no one will ever love me back? Someone will love my soul? You know just as well as I do how pointless all this talk of souls is."

"Well... I'm not exactly stopping traffic, either."

He says this with such a serious face that I can't keep from laughing.

"There was one," I say eventually. "A guy with a tattoo on his neck, right here. I saw him every day by my building. He'd be there when I went out. I don't know who he was waiting for, but I wanted it to be me. Sometime in the future, you know? I walked past him a thousand times, but he never so much as glanced at me. Not once. I kept telling myself that this time, today, he'd walk up and start talking to me. This went on for a few weeks. And then he disappeared. He must have met whoever he was waiting for. For a long time after that I hoped he'd come back. I'd think about him and make all kinds of stupid plans. I thought that he was the one person I could be with my whole life... Now, of course, I don't think that. I didn't actually know him at all. Might be the same for you and me. We're a lot alike. We both live in imaginary worlds. That's what my mom says. You imagine one for me, and I imagine one for you..."

"You've never thought that... that we... that we could, uh... be together?"

A charge fills the air in the room as it does before a storm, and I know that something is happening. We are sitting together and looking into one another's eyes. Our faces are so close, but neither of us looks away. When this happens in the movies people start kissing, but in real life I jump to my feet.

"Back in a minute."

I wander the streets aimlessly. It's cold and I could do with a smoke, but I haven't brought my coat or cigarettes because I said I wouldn't be long.

I see a stray dog limping on one foot. I feel sorry for him. I want to pet him, give him some food and a hot cup of tea and ask, "Hey, dog. What else have you lost, apart from your owners?"

I do bend down to him and ask, but of course he doesn't answer.

I see light in some of the windows of this small town, which means that I'm not the only one awake at this hour.

I see two trees whose branches are entwined and whose crowns are leaning together. I want to ask them if they like it that way. But the trees can't answer me.

I see a drunk slumped against a wall. He is asleep. His head is hanging low and he's having trouble breathing. Ordinarily I can't stand these people, but for some reason I feel sorry for him.

I see a small creek and wonder what great and wide river it flows into.

I start shivering. I'm really feeling the cold. I look for the homeless dog but I can't remember how to get to the place where he was. So I go back to the hotel. The lights are off in our room, and he is sleeping with his back to me. He's pretending to be asleep. I'm sure he's been waiting for me. The moment I sit down on the edge of the bed, he turns over.

"Hey, what happened?" he asks. "You're shaking."

I really am shaking, though I only notice it then. He takes me in his warm arms and tries to comfort me… and I say something incoherent about a homeless dog and some trees, but I'm sure he understands. Of course he understands. He always does.

I can't remember how I fell asleep... probably like that, in his arms, still muttering something as I drifted off.

7

At some point – I'm not really sure when – our journey starts to turn into a nightmare. We're getting on one another's nerves, getting irritated, fighting for no reason, shouting at one another. Like a couple who have been living together for twenty years. During these fights we'll go for hours without speaking. Sometimes I just hate him.

I'm driving and I'm on edge. Really on edge. To the point of hating him. He hates me, too, and for the same reason – just because. We've probably been spending too much time together. Maybe we'd never really been such good friends if we're fighting like this. I can see him getting angry; I can see it in the expression on his face, his gestures, his eyes, his crooked smile. I know him all too well. I know that when his eyes narrow just like that and he sticks his chin out, he's really angry. At me. Who else? We've been together for so long now. He closes his eyes, and I know he's trying to fall asleep because he doesn't even want to see me, let alone talk to me. I step on the accelerator as tears well up in my eyes. There's only one thought: I can't let him see me crying.

We arrive at another town. He's still sleeping, or at least pretending to. I drive around in search of a cheap hotel and stop at a movie theater. I stare straight ahead into the distance, gripping the wheel tightly. I am not in this car anymore. I'm somewhere far away: not sure where exactly, but it's definitely a place where I don't feel like hating my best friend, maybe even a place where there is no best friend. Or anyone else.

"Hey, what's up with you?" he asks suddenly.

"Let's go see a movie," I suggest, still looking ahead.

"Sure, why not."

We get out of the car and walk to the theater. A film has just started. Two teenagers are kissing in the back row. No one else is there. I'm not even looking at the screen, just staring ahead as if it's not really there. I don't know how long I've been like that, staring into nothingness, but it is his touch that finally brings me back to life.

"I feel bad," he says.

"Me too," I reply.

"It's not like you think... you see, you're my best friend, but... something's grown between us. I don't know how to explain it."

"I know what you mean," I say. "Perfectly." I turn toward him and look straight into his eyes. In the dark theater I can barely see them, but I can feel his hot breath and the warm touch of his hand. He's holding my hand. This gesture suddenly becomes so sweet and familiar that my heart bursts and I finally get it: he is the one. My second me. We're out of this world, and we have to savor everything that we have right now – these fleeting moments – before we return to real life.

This is when he kisses me. I kiss him back: it's not bad, not at all. I think there is nothing better in the world than this. There was one time that I looked at him and saw my own ugly reflection. How could I kiss *that*? Now I open my eyes, but it doesn't change the way I feel at all. As we tear ourselves away from one another, we each stare at the other and see our own reflections. We've discovered something. Two separate discoveries, but they amount to the same thing: We are drawn to one another. We are more than just friends. I don't know when it started, but it wasn't just now, and it wasn't back when we were skipping class and listening to rock. So what if he's not the kind of guy girls fall in love with? So what if I'm not the kind of girl boys fall in love with? When people see us together they'll probably make a snide face and say – to themselves, behind our backs, or even directly to us – that we really do suit one another and that we won't ever find anything better. But why spend your entire life looking for something better, thinking that what we have is not good enough for us? We really have found one another. You could even say we are lucky. Other people look for ages without finding this.

We leave the car at the theater and walk to the hotel hand in hand. It's a good thing the town is so small and the hotel isn't far away. We go up to the room and make love until morning.

This is the first time for both of us, but since we know each other so well, our first time is as perfect as a first time can ever be. I kiss every inch of his body, his thin, pale, unattractive body. But this doesn't bother me. Despite his apparent ugliness, I feel a desire for him. He kisses me: my lips, my hands, my breasts. We feel one another's every movement and become completely absorbed by our sensations. No one in the world is happier than us. No one is more beautiful. In our own little world we are perfect. I look at his body and his face and am surprised to think: how could I not notice how handsome he is? He whispers almost deliriously: "You are so beautiful!"

It is morning.

I'm sitting with my back to him, curled up in the covers with my knees to my chest, smoking.

"What now?" I ask.

"I don't know," he says. "I love you."

"I love you too."

"What's going on?"

"I was thinking the same thing. There's no way this could have happened at the beginning."

"That's why we became friends."

In part we're trying to reassure ourselves that because we have no past there will be no future. In a couple of days we have to separate, and we don't know for how long. That was our first thought, but neither of us is brave enough – or perhaps we're both too strong – to back down now.

"She'll be lucky to have you." I say.

"Who?"

"The girl you're going to be with, the one you'll fall in love with."

"What we have now won't happen again."

"Probably not."

I sit with my back to him while he lies there staring at the ceiling, and we talk about things we never talked about before. We joke and laugh. He's become part of me, and I've become part of him. We're like Siamese twins, or – better still – the same person. I know him better than I do myself. And now I don't understand myself at all. His feelings are mine: his pain is mine, and so is his joy. We've just traded everything. It doesn't seem like this can happen. But I can tell you that this is exactly what happened.

8

He's driving. I can't do it. My hands are shaking and I'm on the verge of tears. From the very beginning I promised myself that I wouldn't cry, that we were just saying goodbye – that doesn't mean anything – but it's not easy to hold back.

When I get home I'm going to get a job and take night classes. I'm going to start living an ordinary life like everyone else. Whether he's mine or not isn't all that important. I'm used to being on my own, so this won't keep me back. This, in any case, is what I thought at the very beginning. Even when he said that he was staying in this town for a while – and that he may not ever return – I was calm. If he wants to stay, let him, a true friendship can only be proven by time and distance. But at some point everything changed. Things weren't like they were before. It happened at some elusive point: it wasn't even when we had sex, but much earlier. I look for that moment, try to find and capture it in the dark alleys of my memory. But that's not important now. What is important is that we're about to say goodbye and I'll be alone again. Just like before.

And... the sun above me. It has only just risen: slow and lazy. The sun is especially soft today. It spreads out over this sleeping town, which is beautiful in its own way. I find it unpleasant though. I'd never seen it before, not in pictures, not on television, but in my own imagination I visualized these streets and buildings, these little cafés and the pizzeria. There isn't even a McDonalds here. I can picture the two most popular music stores: basically the same as we have at home, in basements, with a motley assortment of posters on the walls. I can even imagine the clerks in these shops. In a month or so they'll already know my friend by name and set aside interesting albums especially for him. But it seems he hasn't thought about any of this. He's looking at the city joyfully and hopefully. A new life awaits him here.

We're holding hands, and suddenly there's a lump in my throat. I don't notice the tears running down my face. The first time in my life. At first I don't even understand what's happening. And he, it seems, has completely forgotten about me and our hands.

"Now you can go home," he said. "That's it. We made it."

"It's not fair!" I blurt this out like a child. "I'm not going anywhere without you!"

"Come on," he says. "Tell me, what would we do together now? What are we? Friends? Lovers? Enemies? There were times I hated you so much, and at other times I loved you more than life itself."

"But maybe we can start over again? We could pretend that we don't know one another, that there was no bartender or that girl in the high heels, or Angela, or that guy with the tattoo... that we didn't spend that night together!"

"It wouldn't work," he says.

Now I start sobbing. There's no stopping me, and I can taste the salt in my tears.

"You'll find someone else," he says. "This isn't really love, you know." He's trying to calm me, but he has no idea that these aren't the words I want to hear.

"And will I find a friend?" I ask. "Maybe it's not love, but our friendship."

"Was that really friendship?" he asks. "We were both outcasts. We were the weirdos. We didn't listen to their music or wear the same clothes as them. They hated us, that's what made us close. Do you think we'd have become friends if either of us had known anyone else?"

"We would have... I know it."

"And I know we wouldn't have. You wouldn't have even taken a second look at me."

It took me a long time to stop crying. He tried to carefully pull his hand out from mine, but I gripped it even tighter.

"No, I don't remember anything... I don't want to remember, I won't let you go... We didn't agree to this, you said you were just staying awhile, you never said it was for ever."

"All the same, I'm going. Got it?"

I get into the car, look around, start the engine, and set off. In the mirror I see him still looking at me, he might even be crying. I'd like to think so. It's so strange traveling without him. Without always hearing his laugh, smelling his smell. The radio plays the same song. I drive back through thousands of conversations: about his father, my family, love and friendship, dances and stars, Radiohead and Blur. I drive back through bottles of wine, liters of beer and cocktails, and countless packs of cigarettes. I drive back past thousands of signs and billboards, all of them the same or just similar-looking, I drive past all the same acquaintances, all the same towns we stopped in, I drive past the roadside cafés where we had lunches and breakfasts, where we argued and laughed together. I can sit in these places for hours, staring out the window and drinking cup after cup of awful coffee. I don't mean anything to anyone, just like it used to be. And no one means anything to me. I drive past the town where we changed or, perhaps, where we became ourselves, and I take a long walk along the embankment and stand in front of the club.

On the road I sometimes try to imagine what he's doing at this exact moment, but nothing ever comes of it. Whenever I try to remember those streets, cafés, and music shops that I pictured before, I can't ever remember them... sometimes it's hard to remember things you've seen or felt, and remembering something you've never seen before is far more difficult. Impossible, in fact.

Tragedies are taking place somewhere in the world. People encounter one another in the street so that a wild love can flare up and go out, making one of them, or maybe both, suffer. Somewhere people are having sex: with those they love or don't love, with one person or several, they fall asleep in one another's arms or fall apart once and for all. Someone is crying in the bathroom or into a pillow, someone else is sleeping peacefully or waking up to go to work. Someone is killing someone else: in thought, with a glance, or in fact. Someone is listening to rock, someone else is listening to alternative, and someone is drinking in a bar and listening to jazz. Someone is smoking, and someone else is putting on a nicotine patch. Someone is cursing, or loving, or hating, or despising someone else. In general, people live, do stuff, feel things, and keep hoping. And I'm the only one who's driving a battered old Lada, existing apart from all this, beyond all feeling and thought, entirely alone. Nothing to distract me but the wheel. I'm not me anymore. I'm hardly aware of what's happening around me because I haven't been sleeping much. At night I'm driving or sitting in 24-hour cafés, and during the day I wander the streets.

In a word – I'm going home.

I don't know how many days it took me to get back because I didn't count them. Time stopped. I'd sometimes pull up in the middle of nowhere and stay there until it became morning or night. Or leave the car in a lot somewhere and go wander in a strange town, wiping the tears away.

I don't know where he is now. I rarely think about him. I'm not even sure if he really existed. More and more the past resembles a dream.

I don't live with my parents anymore. When I get home from work I feed my fat cat. I have a lot of friends: people don't think I'm strange. From time to time men turn up, and they fall in love with me or pretend to. But the first person to believe in me, who didn't push me away, who made me love and feel, was my best friend. And if you ask me now whether I would like to go back to being that plain and gloomy schoolgirl but with him at her side, then you would hear me say: yes, I would.

You might ask, of course, what happened to him. I don't know. Maybe he went into business or joined a rock band, or maybe he became a regular family man with a few kids and a housewife. Maybe he died, I don't know… But all I need to do is close my eyes and think about him, and right away I'm back in that car being blown around by the cool wind, my head stuck out of the window, with him next to me.

"Hey, what's coming up next? Take a look at the map, will you?"

Translated by Christopher Tauchen

Book Avenue

BOOK AVENUE

When I went back there – the one and only time – the café was gone. Vera had sold the business several years before, and the new owners had been unable to turn a profit. The ruined Book Avenue, long in the red, had closed its doors. The new owners sold out to still newer owners who turned it into a Chinese restaurant.

The café's sign was gone, but the red Chinese lamps were still in place above the entrance. The steel door leading downstairs was slightly ajar, as if inviting me to look inside and remember the good old days. But I couldn't bring myself to go down. I wanted to keep remembering the café as it had been before, back when things were good.

Cigarette smoke stung your eyes the moment you went in. The ventilation was awful, and everyone smoked too much. The lighting also left much to be desired: the café was in a windowless half-basement, and darkness reigned even during the day. In the first room – the smoking section – there was a bar and a few stools. A door led to a second room where there was a TV and some lounge chairs, but no one ever went there. The entire place was decorated with bamboo: the bar, the walls, the picture frames; even the placemats were made of worn bamboo that had long since lost its luster. Scenes of Caribbean beaches were painted on the walls in shades of green. Several portraits of Bob Marley hung in the corners, and a yellow-green-black Jamaican flag was pinned up on the wall across from the entrance. Soft reggae music kept up the theme. The place may have seen better days, but this is how I remember it.

Book Avenue had never been that popular. The only people who went there were the regulars, though the place did achieve cult status in certain circles. People held parties and birthdays there. Everyone knew everyone else, and in the evening you could see Vera, the owner, moving from table to table and stopping to chat with her patrons. On especially busy nights she was happy enough to don an apron and take their orders, bring them food, and clear their dirty dishes.

We'd go there every night and stay until close, as if there were nothing else for us to do. We had tea or coffee, sometimes something stronger. We smoked. We talked about anything and everything, or we just sat there saying nothing. We never tried to find a particular reason for our being there, but I'd say there was one all the same.

There were five of us: Lola (Lola wasn't her real name, of course, but that's what we called her. I can't remember who thought it up or why, but the name was surprisingly fitting); Rusik (short for Ruslan); Sima (which he claimed was what it actually said in his passport: we never checked); and Max, the only one with an ordinary name. And me, of course: my name is Eva.

Lola: a pair of arresting blue eyes that looked like the sea on a clear morning, and blond curls like an angel in a picture. She complained that no one listened to her because they were lost, mouths agape, in her eyes. I think she was flattered by the attention. She considered herself an avant-garde artist. God knows what that meant. To avoid looking stupid, we never asked, and she never offered an explanation. I never saw any of her work (Did it even exist?) but I did like the doodles she made on the backs of paper napkins at the café. She did this constantly.

Rusik was sweet and cheerful, the happiest one of us all. His jokes rode the line between wit and pure filth, and when he got carried away he came off as obnoxious and arrogant. Most of the time he just made us laugh, and we would forget how intolerable he could be. His hair was cut short, and he wore old hooded sweatshirts that were either hand-me-downs from his older brothers or something he'd picked up second-hand.

Max wore a long coat and loved the Beatles. He was the most mysterious character in our group at that time. Something always seemed to be eating at him. We couldn't work out what it was, and he never felt the need to let us into his strange inner world.

And as for Sima: he was just himself. Nothing more, nothing less.

We never went to the movies or to nightclubs. None of us knew where the others lived or what they did when we weren't together. We didn't even know if anyone was using their real names. When the café closed for the night we'd stand outside for a while, keeping up the conversation in the fresh night air, and then each of us would set off in our own direction, careful to see that our paths did not cross.

To other people we looked like a regular group of teenagers who had nothing to do and needed to get a life. Actually, we were all unique – or at least that's what we wanted to believe. If we were focused on a single idea we could work well together. Had we all been able to sing or play instruments, we definitely could have started a band. If we'd all been able to draw, we could have held exhibitions or become animators. If we'd all been able to write, we could have published a poetry collection and organized readings.

But we all had our own directions, our own ideas. We were all so caught up in ourselves that we took no interest in what the others were doing.

"Listen to this," said Sima. He started to read from the book in his hands. *"The most important thing I learned on Tralfamadore was that when a person dies he only* appears *to die. He is still very much alive in the past, so it is very silly for people to cry at his funeral. ... When a Tralfamadorian sees a corpse, all he thinks that the dead person is in a bad condition in that particular moment, but that the same person is just fine in plenty of other moments.* That's good stuff, isn't it?" And with that he gulped down the last of his coffee.

Sima adored Vonnegut. He liked to read out passages from his books and then say: "That's good stuff, isn't it?" Perhaps we really did think Vonnegut was good stuff. Or maybe Sima just picked the good quotes. In any case, we always agreed with him.

"Anything avant-garde is so trendy nowadays." Lola would talk on and on about things we knew nothing about. "I mean, collectors will pay anything for a Malevich or a Kandinsky."

"The Beatles transformed pop culture into art. The band's a legend and it always will be." That, of course, would be Max.

"What do you think? Is the world really going to end like the Mayans predicted, or is it all a hoax?" We never knew what to expect from Rusik. Even when he started out on something serious, he'd always manage to turn it into something absurd.

So that's how it was: Sima read, Lola drew on napkins, Max listened to the Beatles, Rusik joked, and I spent my time hoping that our café would get a jukebox so we could choose any song we wanted. If there was anything I could talk about with the same enthusiasm that Sima had for his Vonnegut, it was that jukebox.

If I were an artist I could depict this place with paints and pencils; if I were a director I could make a film about it. But right now I'm lacking words, epithets, and metaphors to accurately convey just how unique this café was, this place that seemed perfectly ordinary at first glance, nothing special. When you talk about it – like I'm doing now – there is so much that remains out of view, like the energy that hovered somewhere above our favorite table under the flag. Though maybe it was just a cloud of smoke?

At first it was just me and Sima – had it not been for us, there wouldn't have been any others. We were the first to come to this place and the first to find ourselves at the same table. That day I just happened to drop by: I was drawn to the sign with the unusual name, Book Avenue. Sima looked up at me and, even though we didn't know each other, said:

"Listen to this: *We were aware of all the comedy in this. But, as brilliant as we were when we put our heads together, we did not guess until we were fifteen that we were also in the midst of a tragedy. We thought that ugliness was simply amusing to people in the outside world. We did not realize that we could actually nauseate strangers who came upon us unexpectedly.*

We were so innocent as to the importance of good looks, in fact, that we could see little point to the story of "The Ugly Duckling," which I read out loud to Eliza one day – in the mausoleum of Professor Elihu Roosevelt Swain."

"What's that?" I asked, confused.

Sima was amazed and looked at me as if seeing me for the first time, which was indeed the case.

"In what sense? I was just reading from this book, I didn't mean anything by it."

We made no arrangements to come back the next day, but we came back anyway. And so it started: every night we'd part like strangers and the next day we'd greet each other like old friends. Max joined us after a while.

We were struck by his appearance: wavy hair that fell over his eyes, pale bloodless lips, a Beatles T-shirt, a thin torso clothed in a long heavy coat, an absent stare – he was certainly not of this world.

He sat alone at the next table drinking mineral water.

"Hi!" said Sima. "Beatles?" He pointed at the T-shirt.

Max smiled bashfully. "I like them."

"So do we," said Sima.

That was enough to get him going. Max started to talk and kept talking for a long time, but it wasn't boring, so even Sima forgot about his Vonnegut and listened to the tale of this legendary band. Max moved to our table and sat there until late that night. He came again the next day and sat with us. No need to ask.

Lola and Rusik joined our group later. I can't remember how Rusik got there. Maybe I wasn't there at the time, or maybe it was that he fit in so easily and naturally that it seemed as if he'd always been with us.

I was the one who met Lola first. There weren't any free tables, so she asked if she could join me: "Is anyone sitting here?" – "My friends are coming soon, but you're welcome to stay if you don't mind interesting company." – "And what if *they* mind me being here?" I took a look at this beautiful girl and smiled, shaking my head: "They definitely won't mind."

Indeed, the boys required no explanation at all.

Sometimes if I arrived early Vera would come sit and chat

with me at our table under the flag. She'd light a cigarette, push the hair out of her eyes, and say:

"I can't do this anymore."

She'd tell me how she hired a new cook who burned the meat. Or about how they'd run out of alcohol with a whole group of thirsty birthday revelers and she had to send a waitress for a new supply. She told me in confidence that they were updating the menu and asked which dishes could stay and which should go. Then she told me that she'd been talking to a graphic designer about a new sign, but that she still wasn't sure whether it was worth changing. That was when I asked her why the café was called Book Avenue.

"You know, that's such an old story. There used to be a second-hand bookshop here, and the sign stayed. We've been meaning to change it – we even went to see a designer – but there are so many papers to sign. It's not as easy as it seems. And besides, everyone's used to it."

"I didn't know about that. About the bookshop, that is."

"That's because you weren't even born then."

"What happened to it?"

"No one knows. It was just abandoned. Some of the books are still down in the lower basement. It's pretty damp down there. The books are falling apart, but I can't bring myself to get rid of them."

"Are there many?"

"Loads. I don't know what to do with them. I could try to sell them, but what good are they to anyone? A library wouldn't take them in that state."

"Would you mind if we looked at them sometime?"

"Sure, but they're not much to look at! You can take whatever you want."

The lower basement smelled of damp and old books: the smell of antiquity and the previous century. A small room was crammed with boxes. I took a book at random – its title and author meant nothing to me – and started leafing through the damp pages. I was struck by this smell of old, quietly dying books. I looked around: the others were doing the same. We picked up books like treasures on an archeological dig. And to us they were indeed treasures. What could be more mysterious than a collection of old books in a secret, invisible basement? Books with unknown authors and titles, books that could be about anything.

We stayed all afternoon, we'd lost track of time, moving from one stack to the next, skimming through individual books or examining entire stacks by their covers. The dim light made it difficult to make out the words, but reading the books was not at all necessary. We breathed them in, mechanically flipping through the pages.

"It's hard to believe," I said, breaking a long silence that was disturbed only by rustling pages, "that there could be such a mysterious place in our town."

One time Lola told us that her parents had sent her to a therapist. From then on, for no reason at all, she would suddenly start telling us about her sessions in detail. We thought her stories were funny, but she took offence whenever we didn't take her seriously.

"My parents think I'm antisocial. Me? Antisocial? And this comes at a time when I've always got plenty of people around me. Especially guys. It's easier to get to know guys."

"But your parents must have some reason to think that," observed Sima.

"Sure, it was my drawings, first of all. But what really made them lose it was when I painted my room black. Right away they just knew I was a sociopath! All because I didn't want pink or blue! It's completely illogical. To hell with them. I don't pretend to be completely with it, but I don't want to be shut up in a loony bin."

"Not a chance," said Rusik, smiling. "You couldn't be crazy with eyes as beautiful as yours."

Lola said nothing, and I wondered: Is she making this up?

We were at our table playing tic-tac-toe on a paper napkin. Rusik and I were losing 9-0 to Lola and Max, so it was a complete surprise when Max, who had been absorbed with the game suddenly froze and stared off into the distance. We could see that he was watching a girl who had just walked in.

"What's she doing here?" Max said to himself.

"Who is she?" asked Rusik.

Max did not answer.

We all stopped playing and watched the girl and her companion. He was drinking from a large tankard of dark beer and smoking a cigarette. The girl didn't order anything. She was talking enthusiastically about something, every so often gesticulating wildly. Max couldn't keep his eyes off her. It seemed that he didn't notice the man, but – as I found out later – he'd seen everything just fine.

"Do you know her?" asked Rusik.

"Sort of."

"Why don't you go say hi?"

"Yeah, right," said Max.

"Good call. I'd be scared, too, if I had the same stupid look on my face."

Max watched her and sighed off and on until they left. He wouldn't play tic-tac-toe anymore and only occasionally took a sip of his lukewarm coffee. We soon got tired of taunting him and started talking about something else.

I found Max down in the basement. He was squatting on the floor looking at a book.

"Hey."

He looked up at me and smiled.

"How'd you know I was here?'

"I didn't. I just like coming here. It makes me feel good."

"Me too. Is anyone else here yet?"

"No. You know, I don't think we're the only ones who come down here. This one time I saw Lola on her way back upstairs."

"Yeah, she says this place inspires her."

I smiled and imagined Lola in this darkness, digging out inspiration from the old books. It didn't seem to go well with her image.

"What are you reading?"

Max shrugged and said: "I don't know. I never check.I just grab the first book I find, open it on any page, and start reading."

I didn't ask him any more questions, and he didn't ask me any questions. We talked about something completely different, about what was written in these books, where they came from, and what would become of them.

Everyone was there by the time we went back upstairs, and Lola was again talking about her therapist.

"I'm not going to see him again," she said.

"Really? Weren't you telling us how you adored your doctor?" said Rusik with a smile.

"No need to be nasty, Rusik," she said. "He told me I have to stop coming to these so-called 'evening get-togethers'. How can he ask me to do that? These 'get-togethers,' as he put it, are the only thing that makes me happy, and he knows it."

We said nothing. What was there to say? Oddly enough, Rusik also held his tongue. I was the first to speak.

"Does he think we're a bad influence?"

"Yeah, apparently he can't understand how such different people managed to get together, or why we can't find a normal way to have a good time, like seeing a movie or something."

"What did you say?"

"I said we like it this way. If we really wanted to see a movie, we could go some other time. I never watch movies anyway. I wonder what he means by 'having a good time'."

"What did he say?"

"That I ought to think about it. And that he'd see me again next time."

We had nothing to say. The only sound was Rusik slurping his coffee.

"I don't think us hanging out like this is bad," said Max suddenly.

We looked at him in surprise. I'd have thought it was all the same to Max whether he came here or stayed home listening to the Beatles. The others must have thought the same. So we were all the more surprised when he kept going.

"I mean, it's not like we have much else. At least let us have this one thing."

"That's it, Max!" said Lola. "It's actually good for us! When I see him I'm going to quote you on that."

But Lola didn't come the next day.

Max and I were in the basement talking about Lola. Lately we'd been coming to the café before the others.

"Do you think she'll come back?" he asked.

"I don't know."

She'd been gone for four days, and I couldn't imagine that I'd be worrying so much.

"I don't think anything could've happened to her. She probably just decided to stop coming. That's the right way to do it, just disappear without so much as a word. When it comes down to it, we don't owe one another anything."

"Yes, but… you know, frankly I thought she was a good friend. Probably my only one, even if we only ever saw each other at this café. The amount of time friends spend together isn't the most important thing, right?"

"Sure," said Max. We were quiet for some time before he spoke again. "Anyway, shouldn't we get going? Otherwise Sima will be getting... you know, he's like my best friend."

"And?"

"What do you mean, 'and'? He'll be getting jealous."

"What?"

"Because you're spending all this time with me."

"But listen – I didn't hear this from me." Max walked past me so quickly on his way to the door that my questions about Sima and me never left my lips.

Another five days passed, and still no sign of Lola. We felt dejected and practically didn't say a word to one another. We spent whole evenings buried in our books. I didn't know what was going on. Everything seemed wrong. For some reason we couldn't bear her not being with us.

At some point Rusik suggested that we play his game. We didn't take him seriously at the time, but soon afterwards we were playing it a lot. I kept up the habit for quite a while.

"Let's play a game," said Rusik that first time.

We looked at him and waited to hear what he was suggesting.

"See that woman over there?"

"Yeah." said Max. "So what?"

The woman sat facing away from us at a corner table directly under the portrait of Bob Marley. All that we could see was her majestic ballerina-like posture, dark hair pulled back in a tight bun, and a beautifully sculpted neck with light brown freckles. Perhaps it was a good thing we couldn't see her face. She was doing something strange, something that probably had a particular significance: she would pick up her cup, hold it in place, and then put it back without taking a drink.

"I like doing this when I'm bored," said Rusik. "I choose

someone, whoever's the most interesting, and I make up a story about them. That's it. And we can all tell our own story about them. A person lives only once, only one life, but thanks to us that life takes four different paths, has four different life stories. We don't have to play if you don't want, but lately we've just been sitting around doing nothing. And if we keep going on like this…"

"Fine by me," said Max. "It could be interesting, or at least it won't be boring. But you should go first so we know what to expect."

"Sure thing." Rusik winced as he drank down the last of his coffee, which had already gone cold and bitter. "Here we go: I think she's from a rich family of intellectuals, the conservative kind. From a young age her parents took her to museums and the opera, and she grew up into an educated and cultured young woman. Naturally she went to university, studied something in the humanities. But, as often happens with these kinds of girls, she fell in love with a guy who wasn't part of that crowd, someone who wasn't a good match for her at all. She agonized over this for a long time, trying to convince herself they weren't meant to be. Eventually she let herself be persuaded.

"Then she got married. Not to him, of course, but to a successful lawyer from a well known firm. She's still married to him, but she gave up wearing her wedding ring a long time ago. Maybe she's just taken it off for today. Because that other guy, the love of her life, called and asked her out. And so she's here now, waiting for him. She still doesn't know what will come of this meeting: pain and disappointment, or happiness and a renewed hope that she had lost long ago."

"Sounds like you've been reading too many romance novels," said Sima jokingly. "Your story reminds me of those cheap American dramas, something like *Eternal Love*, or *Don't Leave Me*, or *I'll Never Let You Go*."

Rusik got mad: he grabbed Sima's book and threw it to the side, mumbling something like "whatever." All he was trying to do was to distract us with his story. So what if it was a bit sentimental? He was just saying whatever popped into his head.

"And what do you think?" I asked Sima. "How about your story? It can hardly be any better."

"Hmm. It's obvious, isn't it? She's a prostitute. Not in the literal sense, of course. That's just what I call women who date men because they've got money. One of those men gave her a small studio apartment not far from here, in the center of town. She could say that she's well provided for, but she doesn't have any friends, or anyone who really loves her, or a family. She left her parents a long time ago and doesn't want to think about them because she's ashamed of their poverty. I feel sorry for her. There's nothing romantic about her. Soon she'll grow old and men won't need her any more. That's her tragedy."

"I don't think she's like that at all," I said indignantly. "Where'd you get all that from?"

"Fine, if you've got to have some kind of underlying motive, here you go. Love is impossible for her because the object of her affection is married. She's always the girlfriend. They live next door to one another, they're neighbors. Sometimes they bump into one another at the bakery or in the stairwell. They occasionally spend an evening drinking coffee in her kitchen – "

"There aren't any bakeries around here," said Rusik.

Sima shot him a dirty look and kept going.

"They talk and laugh, and then for several days she isn't herself. Whenever she's with other men, she's still thinking about him."

"That story is by far the furthest from the truth," I said, which was really what I thought. I wasn't trying to get at him, but that's exactly what he thought I was doing.

"You're the one who asked me to tell my story. So I did."

"Easy there," said Rusik. "If we keep going at this rate, this won't be much of a game. The point isn't to get closest to the truth because none of them are going to be anywhere close. The point of the game is that this one woman gets to have four lives, four different life stories. All right?"

"Can't any of you see it?" said Max, who until that moment had been silent: "Doesn't that woman look familiar? It's Lola, only in the future."

That was a good one.

"This woman's life hasn't turned out like she wanted because she's always been too caught up with herself and her problems. She goes to a therapist – that you can see straight away. She probably takes all kinds of pills so she can be happy. She's sad, but she never shows this to other people. She makes herself smile even when she feels like crying. When she was young she dreamed of becoming an artist and was even quite good at drawing, but all of a sudden she stopped and thought: What if it doesn't work out? Now she regrets this and wants to start all over again. But how? – she thinks – I've lived half my life already, maybe more. I could die today or tomorrow. I haven't been able to succeed, so why bother now? But she isn't right to think that way. It's never too late to start again. I wish I could tell her that."

I didn't get a chance to tell my story. The woman got up and walked toward the exit. When she reached the door she looked back at us, grabbed the door handle, and encountered the real Lola.

When Lola sat down at the table, no one asked her about anything. Everyone tried to behave themselves, which was unusual for us. Then Lola asked Vera for "the usual." This was a cappuccino with a dusting of chocolate.

"It's been ages since I've had such good coffee," she

said. Her first sip had left a white ribbon of foam on her upper lip. She licked it off.

"I missed you all so much!" she blurted out. She closed her eyes and rubbed her forehead with the same hand she was using to hold her cigarette. "I doubt you guys missed me all that much."

"We've been waiting for you," said Rusik. "We were worried you might not be coming back."

"I suppose you'd like to know what I've been up to and why I was gone so long."

We all looked at one another.

"You don't have to say anything if you don't want to," Max said.

"I was in the hospital," Lola said.

"Were you sick?"

Lola smiled and took a long drag on her cigarette.

"You could say that. I tried to kill myself."

"What?"

"Well, I slit my wrists. Guys, don't look at me like that, I knew I wasn't going to die. It's just that everyone was getting at me, you know, so I thought I'd give them a bit of a fright. It didn't hurt, wasn't even all that scary. Obviously I knew I wasn't going to die. And besides, I'm a creative type, we're allowed to have breakdowns. Sometimes I just get so… I felt so awful, and on top of everything… well, forget it."

"And here I am thinking you're an optimist," said Rusik. "I thought you were like me."

Lola smiled: "Please don't be mad at me!"

"We'll have to think about it," said Sima as he thumbed through his book. "Listen to what Vonnegut has to say about this: *I won't know myself until I find out if* life *is serious or not,'said Trout. It's* dangerous, *I know, and it can hurt a lot. That doesn't necessarily mean it's* serious, *too.*"

We listened to Sima as he read. We were used to hearing

Vonnegut's opinions and always gave his words a lot of weight.

That's when I wondered whether I ought to believe Lola. She looked pretty well rested and tan for someone who had been laid up in a hospital. We didn't know anything about one another except for the stories we told. They could be real, or they could be lies. There was no way of finding out. Lola wasn't quite as pessimistic as she wanted to appear.

We knew when Sima started to smile that we were going to hear something interesting. He stopped staring at his book and said:

"Here, listen to this: *She improvised around the music of the Pullman porter's son: she went from liquid lyricism to rasping lechery to the shrill skittishness of a frightened child, to a heroin nightmare. Her glissandi spoke of heaven and hell and all that lay between. Such music from such a woman could only be a case of schizophrenia or demonic possession.*" Sima read slowly, exaggerating the stresses and pauses.

"Hold it, what's a glissandi?" asked Lola.

"It's fluid transition from one note to another," said Max. "A musical term."

"What, do you spend your spare time reading all sorts of encyclopedias?" Rusik joked.

"Sometimes," Max said. He wasn't joking.

"Here, listen to the rest! *My hair stood on end, as though Angela were rolling on the floor, foaming at the mouth, and babbling fluent Babylonian.*"

"What's that from?" asked Max.

"*Cat's Cradle.*"

"But you were reading something else last time," said Rusik. He almost seemed offended by this, though I'd have thought him the least interested in Sima's readings.

"Really?" said Sima. "You're right, I was reading from *Slaughterhouse Five*. That one has a few good bits, too."

"Maybe you could read from the same one so the stories and quotes don't get mixed up in my head," said Lola.

"I suppose. I have trouble myself remembering what I'm reading every day."

"But haven't you already learned it all by heart?" asked Rusik. A smug grin lit up his face as he got ready to laugh at this joke.

"I can remember a few parts, of course."

"You shouldn't be so hung up on just one writer."

Sima shrugged: "Says who?"

"The thing is," said Rusik, "we've all got our quirks. If we didn't, we probably wouldn't be sitting here together."

"You're right," I said. "We're in an exclusive club, for people with quirks."

"But why do you like Vonnegut so much?" Lola asked Sima. "I'd just like to know. He writes some kind of science fiction, doesn't he?"

"Not really. He doesn't write science fiction, it's just that he moves from reality to something unreal. That's how he arrives at such extreme formats. You see, reality is very simple and present, nearly autobiographical, and then all of a sudden his characters encounter completely extraordinary things, stuff that could never happen in real life."

"Sort of like how in one of his books the narrator grants freedom to his character, that is, he completely erases the boundaries, like you were saying."

"You've read *Breakfast of Champions*?" said Sima, surprised.

"I can't remember what it was called," I lied.

In fact, it had been a long time since I'd read all the books he loved.

Max worked at a music store called Sgt. Pepper's, or at least that's what he told us. I believed him, in any case. He said that he dreamed of traveling to Liverpool, the Beatles' hometown, but that he could never afford it on his small salary. If you could have a soundtrack for evry person like they do in the movies, then this would be the moment to cue "Yesterday." That's Max's song. That's the song I was listening to in my head that night when Max told me about the girl who had come to the café.

He'd seen her once when she dropped by the music store to ask about an album.

"For the life of me I can't remember the band she was looking for. She just blurted out a bunch of names and said, 'Do you have this? What about this?' She bought three or four CDs, and after a couple days she came back again. I still see her a lot, sometimes in the shop, sometimes outside, on Kirov Street or by the fountains. She's always showing up right before my eyes. Like it was on purpose. Beautiful, though, isn't she?"

I nodded.

We sat quietly for a long time. It seemed like he'd forgotten that I was sitting there next to him, that we'd been talking, that he even existed, so I was startled when he began talking again.

"I wonder what it would be like if people couldn't feel anything. No pain, no regret, no insult, no shame."

"But if people didn't feel those things, then there also wouldn't be love, joy, or happiness either."

"I'd like that: not to feel anything. It seems simpler that way. If someone offered that to me, if they said, 'Hey Max, take this, it works right away, and you won't feel anything ever again,' I'd say yes without a moment's hesitation."

"Is it really that bad?"

"Yes."

"Nothing to be done about that. Think about what you'd be missing without those other feelings. Like happiness."

Max sighed. "You know what? You can't miss something you've never had."

I thought he was exaggerating and I smiled: "It just seems like that, that you feel bad."

"No, I'm serious" – even though we could barely see one another in the darkness, at that moment he looked straight into my eyes – "You have no idea what it's like."

I realized that was not only what he thought, but also the way he actually felt. I also understood that he was in a very bad place, and that there was nothing I could do to help. There probably wasn't anyone who could. And at that moment I became conscious of all of mankind's weaknesses on a global scale. No matter what I said, however optimistic or positive, none of it could have done a thing.

When we came up from the basement, Vera was sitting at our table. She put out her cigarette and smiled.

"Hey."

We sat down and ordered coffee and something to eat.

"Well, guys, I've got some news for you."

"What is it?"

"I'm thinking about what to do with the café. I'm moving to Moscow soon, and for good. So now I've got a decision to make."

"What about?"

"Whether to sell the café or do something else with it. Maybe I could hire someone to run it."

"So you're not going to be here anymore?" I asked.

"No," she said, shaking her head, "I'm not going to be here anymore."

When Vera left the table, the rest of us could barely say a thing. Max sat there, sad and dejected. It had turned out to be an exceptionally unfortunate night. Sima's disappointed gaze darted between me and Max, Lola was mumbling something about herself, and Rusik was drinking beer on his own, sighing without end. I still hadn't realized then what I would discover later: this was one of the worst nights not only in my time at the café, but in my entire life. That night was the beginning of the end.

All things must come to an end; our meetings also couldn't last forever. We had a good time, and we'd have given our lives for one another: we knew this. At the same time there was something wrong, something unnatural about our meetings. And so, all of it ended just as it began: one fine day it was just me and Sima. The first to go was Rusik, who said he was moving. Then an embarrassed Lola told us that she was leaving to go to art school in another city. For a long time afterwards three of us would meet: me, Max, and Sima. But after a while Max stopped coming. Then there were two of us. Rumors that Vera had decided to sell were confirmed. We hoped that nothing would change even after this, but we hoped in vain. When the deal was finally made, and Vera left, we still went to Book Avenue for a while. But everything had changed in a way we couldn't quite detect, and it wasn't as nice and cozy as it had been. We both made new friends and started new relationships, so there was no need for us to continue our friendship.

On that last night in the café, it seemed as if nothing had changed. A cloud of smoke hung over our table under the flag, the ashtray was piled high with cigarette butts, and a copy of *Slaughterhouse Five* lay in front of us next to three cups, two filled with cold coffee and one with plain old water.

"I never meant to hurt you," said Sima.

"I know." I looked him in the eyes.

"Want to play?" he said. "For the last time?"

"Sure. You first."

"All right. Past, present, or future?"

"Your choice."

"Future it is, then." Sima got quiet and thought about what he was going to say. Then he lit a cigarette and began telling his story: "I don't think she'll ever lead a normal life. By which I mean a normal family with two kids and a husband who goes off to work every day. That's not for her. But all the same, she won't be alone: there will always be a place where she can go and where someone is waiting for her. Not in this café, but something very similar. She'll sit at a table, drink cold coffee, reminisce about her life, and think about the future. She will travel a lot. Not just to other countries, but to ordinary towns at home. She won't be able to stay in one place or with one man."

"What, so there's not going to be anything good in her life?"

"What do you mean? She has life itself. I never said that she didn't like life. And even though she'll never know it, she'll always have a person who loves her and who thinks about her. 'May she be well, wherever she may be.'"

"I don't think it will be like that. She's not one of those women who men fall in love with for life. Of course they all say they do at the beginning, but then a few months go by and they forget about her. They all forget. As if she'd never existed. Like a person wiped from the face of the earth. You see, she's not the kind of person who people fight for or jump off roofs for. She's not the kind of girl that people remember all their lives."

"But he isn't the kind of person who forgets."

"Do you want to hear his story?"

"Go ahead."

"I think he's going to become a great man. Not famous, just great. He will achieve much in his life, and have status in society. And, of course, he will have a family. Because it couldn't be any other way. He will never find himself at rock bottom. And he will love his family. Especially his children. One of them might be a girl who he names after the girlfriend from long ago. Or maybe not. She may just disappear from his memory. But to tell the truth, that's not what I'd want to happen.

We looked at one another for a long time in painful silence.

"Who's going to go first?"

"Let me stay," I said.

"As you wish," he said, smiling.

"You know," I said impulsively, "we would've made a good couple."

He smiled.

"I know. We would've been good together. Strange, but good."

"I wonder what Vonnegut would have to say about it."

"He'd say: *Love does not seem important to me. What does seem important? Bargaining in good faith with destiny.* And that was the one time I disagreed with him."

Sima got up, leaned forward, kissed me on the lips, and walked to the door. I watched him go. Some things are better left unseen. Watching him leave was one of those things. I thought then that I would remember him turning his back to me my whole life.

The feeling of Total Loneliness came over me like a wave. I suddenly felt so sad I could have cried. My hands trembled, and I broke out in a cold sweat. "It was bound to happen sometime," I thought. "And now it has. I didn't do anything to cause it – didn't choose the day, didn't push him – I just waited for it, afraid of the moment it would finally come."

Mindlessly I spun my cup of coffee this way and that,

brought it up to my lips, and then set it down again without drinking. Then I lit a cigarette and immediately stubbed it out. I remembered that woman who we invented stories for, and I understood the root of her misfortune: on that day she was overcome by the feeling of Total Loneliness.

I don't know how long I sat there like that. A long time, probably, because it was already dark when I left. As I was leaving I said goodby to Olga, who had stayed on even after the change in ownership.

"See you tomorrow," she said.

"See you tomorrow," said I.

Translated by Christopher Tauchen

The Time of My Life

THE TIME OF MY LIFE

1

It all started on New Year's Day; I was lying on the sofa reading the newspaper. I was looking through the travel section to find somewhere to go snowboarding. I like snowboarding. It's for people who are strong, confident, and active, for people who don't want to lie around all day on the sofa, for people who listen to rock and alternative music. I knew full well that I wouldn't be going anywhere and that I'd never take up snowboarding, but all the same I pored over those ads.

The TV was off. From the stereo came the strained voice of Ilya Chert, who was singing about how he "just plays rock." I was singing along and head-banging. I also wanted to stand up straight and yell proudly: "I just play rock." But I don't play rock. I don't play anything.

Someone was at the door. I got up from the sofa and hesitantly dragged myself into the hall, trying to smooth out my messy hair on the way. It was Genka, a neighbor who also happens to be my best friend.

On the day we met I was dancing to Oasis at full volume. The doorbell buzzed, and, without checking the peephole or even asking who was there, I opened the door. I saw an odd-looking guy with shaggy hair, old torn jeans, and a South Park T-shirt worn over a long-sleeved undershirt.

"Uh... hey there," he said.

I stared at him.

"I'm your next-door neighbor. I live right here." He pointed at the door across the way.

"Nice to meet you," I said. "I didn't think anyone had moved in yet."

"I haven't been here long. I'm renting. Listen, uh... What's that you're playing? That's not the Gallagher Brothers, is it?"

"Of course it is," I said.

"Do you suppose I could borrow it sometime? I don't have that one yet..."

So began my friendship with Genka. I heard that he was doing some kind of correspondence course at some university, but I never knew which one. At night he was a bartender at a place called Joy Party, and during the day he either slept or listened to music on his balcony. I often dropped by when he had a night off, and together we would listen to music, drink beer, and smoke. Sometimes he'd teach me how to play his old bass guitar. Sometimes we'd talk, sometimes not; we ate pot noodles and watched hockey on TV.

And now he was standing in front of me with his bass guitar.

"A gift. For New Year's."

"Who's it for?"

"For you, stupid."

"But... it's your bass," I say eventually.

"Yeah, I noticed."

"What is this, some kind of joke?"

Genka sighed.

"I thought I'd buy me a new one for New Year's," he said, "and I figured since you liked this one so much – here, take it. I could never bring myself to sell it. It's like family."

I invited him in, and we celebrated the occasion of my new bass – or rather my "first" – with the end of the cognac, half a bottle of red wine, and a bottle of beer. Then we smoked in the hall, and he went home.

When Genka was gone I looked at the guitar for a long time, ran my fingers over the strings, and slowly plucked them one by one. Then I jumped up. I needed something to do, and fast.

And so I went to Larissa's.

2

Instead of preparing for our exams, we spent January holed up in Larissa's apartment, practicing as late as the building rules would allow. Then we'd go to the store for food and wine, and, once all the wine was drunk and we'd forgotten all about the rules and the neighbors, we'd play again as loud as we could. Even at two in the morning. Thank God we had no amps.

All our lives we'd dreamed of playing in a band: when we watched the Maxidrom music festival on TV, when we went to concerts of rock bands on tour in our town (with their guitars and amps, always looking like they were on something), and when we listened to Billy Joe, who was always saying he wanted us to have the time of our lives.

And then my dream became reality. We'd nearly made it. Larissa wrote the songs and the lyrics, and the favorite in our very small circle was her song "I Love Punk!" I played bass, which I was still learning. Now we needed a guitarist and a drummer, but it wasn't long until a drummer found us himself.

We were sitting and chatting in a corner outside the university assembly hall where no one could hear us. That's where this guy found us. His face was vaguely familiar. Curly hair.

Wide-legged trousers. Some kind of beads around his neck, or maybe not beads, it wasn't clear what those were. An enormous backpack. And huge boots.

"Hi," he said. "I heard you were getting a band together. I play drums."

He paused and waited for some sign of acknowledgment from us. We looked him over.

"What year are you?" asked Larissa.

"First."

"Oh," we both said, disappointed.

On the whole he wasn't that bad. Not too nice to look at, but interesting in his own way. There was something sweet and fun about him, and also something a little unsightly and uncommon.

"He doesn't look like a drummer," I thought. I don't know why I thought this, because I'd never met a drummer before.

"What should we call you?" asked Larissa.

"Kirill."

After class we went to Kirill's place and spent a long time drinking strong black tea without sugar and listening to him play the drums. We decided that he would do, and in honor of this he took us to drink cognac with the first-year students. Of course, they didn't have any cognac, so we had to make do with cheap pre-mixed cocktails out of cans, which were generously provided by the newest member of our band.

3

Genka looked awful. Maybe he was sick, maybe he was hungover. It was always hard to know what was going on with him.

"I stopped by yesterday and the day before, but you weren't here," he said resentfully.

"That's because we're practicing all the time, Genka!" I answered.

"So you've done it, then."

"Done what?"

"Got your band together."

"Just about. We're still missing a guitar, and it doesn't really work without that."

"I'm glad you've got your band. As for the guitar, let me have a think about that. I've got someone in mind. A friend of mine, a good guy. You'd like him. And he can really play."

To mark the occasion, Genka and I decided to go out.

We made it as far as the kiosk outside our building where we bought beer to take back to Genka's. We drank and talked about our promising futures.

We set off in search of our guitarist the very next day.

"He could be anywhere," said Genka as Larissa and I shivered in the cold.

"What does that mean? Where are we even going?" asked Larissa nervously, her scarf wrapped up to her nose.

"He's probably at Partisan, so let's go there."

"What if he's not?" I asked.

"Let's just go to Partisan, and then we can go look for him somewhere else."

"Do we have to do this today?" asked Larissa, whose teeth were now chattering.

Genka looked at her indignantly.

"That's enough of that. Enough with the moaning and groaning and asking stupid questions. Soon we'll be there and you'll know everything."

We fell silent. A trolleybus soon came up to the stop, and we quickly climbed into its warm interior.

Partisan was always packed during concerts. You could see all kinds of people there: girls in heels and miniskirts (not too many, but some); a lot more people in tall black boots, people with pierced noses, eyebrows, ears, and other parts of their bodies, usually drunk or high on something.

We sat down on a bench on the ground floor and smoked. Guys and girls – everyone was smoking. Some smoked cheerfully (these ones laughed together in groups), some smoked listlessly (as if they'd had a date with someone and that person didn't turn up, and so now they were all alone). Perhaps they were waiting for a favorite song, or maybe they weren't waiting for anything and didn't even know how or why they'd ended up here.

Genka left to search the club for the mysterious guitarist. After an hour he found us on a bench opposite the entrance. We were enjoying ourselves, smoking and trying our best to hear the music playing upstairs. The band finished its set, and then we heard the standard Partisan-style music, mostly punk and rock recordings.

"Everyone, this is Billy," said Genka. Next to him was a guy with a Rasta cap and a nose piercing.

"Billy Joe Armstrong?" asked Larissa, obviously pleased with her joke.

He rolled his eyes. "No," he said, "the name's got nothing to do with him. It's a long story. Maybe I'll tell you sometime."

We were half-jokingly talking about the day we'd be the ones on stage when this girl appeared and walked up to Billy. Without so much as glancing at Larissa and me, she pouted her lips and drawled:

"Where have you been? I was getting lonely all by myself. And I keep getting hit on."

Billy looked up at her and let out a deep sigh.

"We can go soon," he said. "Just give me five minutes. I'm in the middle of something."

The girl, still too full of herself to bother looking at us, turned and stomped off in her tall black boots towards the music upstairs.

4

At last, our first practice session: now we could play our own songs with a full band. Vocals, guitar, bass, drums. Larissa, Billy, me, Kirill. As far as I can remember, that session was a complete failure. We messed up, fought, and swore, and it was only at the very end that we managed to muddle our way through the last verse of "I Love Punk!" But afterwards we still went to Larissa's to celebrate. More people showed up, some we knew and others we didn't really know at all. The apartment must have been made of rubber – I still can't work out how it fit so many people. The guys in our band – it was so nice to be able to say that! – drank vodka. Larissa and I drank wine.

When we'd all had our fill, I started singing that last verse of "I Love Punk!" Suddenly I turned to Larissa.

"Wait a minute," I said. "You don't love punk. I mean, it's not a punk you're in love with."

"It's just a song," she said and went out onto the balcony.

It's true, he was no punk. But then, it's hard to say exactly what he was.

Larissa stood on the balcony and looked down. This is the limit, she thought, smiling to herself. She felt like smoking, but she wasn't really a smoker. Larissa was thinking about him: she tried not to – that was easier – but then she'd go and do it anyway. Sometimes it so overwhelmed her that she felt like crying. But she wouldn't cry.

Different crowds, different lifestyles: it wasn't meant to be, she thought. His was a world of techno music and ecstasy, hers was one of punk rock and weed. It just wasn't meant to be.

But what difference does it make being different? All that matters is being together. And if not together, better not to be at all. They'd already given it a try, but nothing came of it. Too bad.

On the outside, everything appeared to be normal: when they ran into one another, they'd say their hellos and moved on. This happens all the time: people nod, keep walking, and forget. So why does it bother her so much? That he doesn't notice her. Or pretends not to. Rushes past without even looking up, lost in some world of his own.

She could go a long time without thinking about him, but then she'd happen to see him somewhere. And as soon as she saw him, it was like she wasn't entirely there. She'd do all the same things she did before – she'd eat, sleep, talk to other people, smile at them – but it wasn't her, because the real Larissa was suffering from pain and happiness at the same time, because the real Larissa could see nothing but him. She hadn't thought such things happened, it really was difficult to believe, even for her. He wouldn't believe it. She knew that he would never believe it. And even if he did, then what? Was it possible to change anything? Of course not. The impossibility of this only made things worse.

She stood frozen on the balcony and looked down as she composed a new song in her head. She was madly in love.

5

I remember this one time when me and Genka are smoking on the balcony – he's smoking weed and I've got a regular cigarette. We're listening to the music inside: "And we'll be together... like Sid and Nancy... Sid and Nancy..."

"I like that song," I say.

"Me too."

We don't say much, just the occasional meaningless exchange.

"How's the band?" he asks.

"Great," I say. "We've been practicing."

As I stub out my cigarette in the ashtray, I notice another one with lipstick on the filter. I point this out to Genka.

At first he smiles like a child, as if glad to see it was still there, but then he frowns and says:

"It's nothing."

"So I guess your love life's going well," I say. I'm trying to cheer him up, but it doesn't work. Genka changes the subject to the song that has by now replaced "Sid and Nancy."

Genka didn't really have a love life! Never had and never will!

She visited him whenever she wanted. Her calls were short: "You home? Not busy? I'll be right over." They'd have sex and fall asleep in each other's arms. Sometimes they'd talk in the kitchen with the lights off, and, even though they couldn't see a thing, they would reach out into the darkness to touch each other's fingers, hair, and face, like they were trying to confirm that they still existed.

In the morning she would leave. She thought that Genka was asleep and couldn't hear her, but he was always just pretending. He'd watch her tiptoe back from the shower, watch her crawl into her sweater, watch her wince slightly as she pulled on her jeans. This was when she did her hair, the moment Genka loved best of all. She had spectacular hair: long and luminous. She would brush it for a long time, then tie it in a knot with an elastic band. After that she would leave, quietly closing the door behind her, and Genka would squeeze his fists as hard as he could. He didn't really know anything about her, not even her phone number: she was always the one who called. He shuddered at the thought that a day would come when she would stop calling. What would he do then? Genka knew perfectly. He'd wait. A month or two, a year, his entire life, until the end of time – she'd have to realize at some point that she was in love with him, too! Because he was in love with her. It couldn't be any other way: if you love someone – truly love them – then that person will love you back. It had to be this way. Otherwise, what's the point?

Now and then Genka was surprised that he saw something in her. You couldn't say that she was all that beautiful or sexy. She'd come over in old jeans, stretched-out sweaters, wrinkled T-shirts. Unattractive, another man might say. Unattractive, they'd write in the glossy magazines. One time Genka read in one of those magazines that girls had to wear something sexy on a date, like a low-cut top or a miniskirt. Sweaters and jeans were only suitable for friendly chats. Genka laughed at the time. He was glad she wasn't like that.

She didn't know why she went to him. Every time she promised herself that would be her last, but when the desire to see him became so strong that she couldn't resist she forgot all about her promises and called that number she knew so well. "You home? Not busy? I'll be right there." What did she need him for? She didn't know anything about him, not where he studied or worked, what his parents did, nothing at all. This all seemed so unimportant and insignificant when they were talking for hours in his tiny kitchen. But during those evenings life itself seemed illusory, somehow unreal, so maybe Genka was also unreal? At a distance from him and that kitchen, she had to admit it: Genka was doing nothing with his life. He wasn't at all suited to be with her, a professor's daughter. She was too good for him. He wasn't a part of her social circle, or her world. In her world she sometimes went to cafes or the theater with other guys. Guys who were like her. They'd take her for ice cream. They'd greet her with roses, as one ought to when going out with a girl. And then she'd give Genka a call.

I am not in love with him, she would think. Not because he's different: it's because I'm not like everyone else.

6

Misha and I were talking about London. If someone had told me that we'd be sitting so close together and talking like regular people, I wouldn't have believed it. But there we were, talking – about London of all places – and chain-smoking. We talked about English books we'd read, about the British pop music we loved so much, about Big Ben and the Houses of Parliament, about the Queen and the princes. I'm not going to say that we had some great spiritual connection – or that I was sitting there thinking only about how handsome he was – but it's not just anyone you can blather on to about London. Sometimes other people would come over to beg money off us for booze. We'd give them whatever we had in our pockets and go right back to talking about London. Maybe we talked about other things, but by the next day all I could remember was that.

"Will we go there someday?" I asked.

He didn't hesitate for a second: "Of course we will!"

I thought, and not for the first time, that I loved him desperately and he knew nothing about it. He had other girls – he'd probably tell them he loved them, and they'd say they loved him, too – while I was nothing: "just a friend."

Winter was coming to an end. We weren't sure if that was a good thing. On the one hand, it would be warm; on the other, spring had a way of getting you down. Spring meant love-stricken couples splashing through puddles, tomcats on the prowl in search of prey, and vitamin deficiency. Instead of enjoying these first warm days and genuine sunlight, everyone was obsessed and overwhelmed with their own problems.

We practiced every day and tried to come up with a name for our band, but nothing came to mind. So we remained just the Band Without a Name.

We were all depressed. Our usual "couple of drinks"

wasn't enough, so we were drinking more and more. Wine, champagne, cocktails, beer. We drank secretly during a lecture. We didn't show up for the next one and instead found somewhere else to go on drinking. In half an hour – with peanuts to chase – we drank our way through a liter of vermouth. But, as the legendary Roma Zver once said: "Vermouth doesn't fix a thing." Every day we drank and made toasts to love, drinking straight from the bottle. Billy and Kirill sometimes smoked weed, but Larissa and I were never interested. We'd try different tobacco flavors or even green tea in our hookah, but we never got a buzz off anything. It's probably a good thing we didn't.

"Tomorrow will be better": so said the purple cartoon rabbit drawn on a wall near our university. And we waited for tomorrow to come. But tomorrow was no better. At least we were done with winter.

PART TWO: SPRING

7

When Billy woke up the clock said 5:30 a.m. He reached over and touched her on the shoulder

"Do we have anything to drink?"

"What?"

"Is there any beer left, or a bottle of water?"

"Shut up, Billy, I'm sleeping."

In a fog she heard Billy let out a deep sigh. Billy. He was bearable only when he was sleeping. That's probably why he slept so little: he liked to piss her off. She let out a sigh of her own and immediately fell back asleep.

The next time she woke up to the smell of fried eggs. Her head was aching and her mouth was dry. She didn't even look in the mirror, just splashed some water on her face and dragged herself to the kitchen, where Billy was busying himself at the stove. She slumped into a chair.

"When did we get back last night?" she whispered.

Billy handed her a glass of water.

"What do you mean, 'we'? Don't you remember? We didn't come back together."

"Really?" She took a sip. "Yuck – what is this?"

"There's aspirin in it. It'll make you feel better. Hungry?"

"No, I'm not..."

She looked at Billy. How does he do it? First thing in the morning and he's already stuffing himself with fried eggs? Billy looked at her closely. His usual smirk was gone. He seemed concerned.

"Are you okay?"

"Don't even ask," she said. "Don't ever let me drink at Korovin's again. I wish I were dead."

"Maybe you should lie down for a bit."

She took his advice and stumbled back to the bedroom. After a few minutes Billy went to her. He sat at her side, and she rested her head in his lap. Billy began stroking her hair, and this made her feel a little better. How wonderful it was sometimes to have him around. Too bad he wasn't often this sweet. And now for the next piece of evidence: only five minutes later, Billy got up and started to get dressed.

"Where are you off to?" she asked as he ran a comb through his hair.

"Got to go. I've got to go see someone."

"Okay, sure. Why so early?"

"I've got to stop off at my place first." Billy tried to change the subject quickly, as he always did when the conversation turned to girls. He stood at the bedroom door somewhat awkwardly. "Well, I'm off. I'll see myself out."

"Go on, then," she said and then looked away.

Billy went outside. It was strange weather: not quite winter, but still not spring. Billy didn't want to go anywhere, but he couldn't stay with her any longer.

You think you can do anything – thought Billy, zipping up his coat and wrapping a scarf up to his ears – but you can't really. Nothing depends on you. Anything you'd want to change couldn't possibly change because of something you did. Say I wanted to live somewhere else, or not see her anymore, or maybe see her, but just have things be different? No, better not to see her at all. Maybe someone in Heaven screwed up something in their Big Ledger… or maybe this is exactly right? And this is just the way it's meant to be? Thoughts like these often came to him, but he never got an answer to the question why he had to suffer this stupid love.

Even that morning, though she was pale without her makeup, with bloodshot eyes and unfamiliar hickeys on her neck, he thought she was the most beautiful girl in the world. The first time they met he barely noticed her: after one quick, indifferent glance, he forgot her face almost immediately. They saw each other a few times in groups, chatted about this and that, argued, and flirted, but even then he didn't think of her as the girl of his dreams. He remembered the night of that party very well. It was one of those parties where everyone got drunk and started kissing, and afterwards she'd be terribly hung over. Together they stood on the balcony and talked. About everything and nothing, whatever came to mind. She would laugh and sometimes think about something to herself without responding right away to what he had said. He remembered what she was wearing that night: baggy jeans with cargo pockets, a white T-shirt with an abstract print, a bracelet on her left wrist, and a wristwatch on her right. She was constantly pushing her short dark hair out of her eyes.

He had a headache the next day, but something important had stuck in his memory, beating its way out from his subconscious: something happened yesterday, something good. He smiled. To this day he continued smiling as he thought about her, even when he was feeling very bad indeed.

8

The web designer leaned back in his chair. Exhausted. His eyes hurt terribly. He looked at his watch: almost 5 a.m. Damn, another all-nighter on the computer. For the millionth time he said it again: I've got to stop working so much. And again the words were forgotten as soon as they left his lips. For some reason he didn't feel sleepy. He glanced at the three empty coffee cups on the desk – there's the reason. And he had to go to class. Might even have to go in early. He tried to remember the days of the week – when's the early class? That's just on Wednesdays. Today's Thursday, so not too early a start. He just needed to sleep a little. If he slept until class he might do okay, though even that wouldn't put him at his best. And he needed to look good, because SHE was coming today. She always went to class on Thursdays. He had to be a bit late so he wouldn't bump into her unexpectedly. Then again, why should he care what she thought of him? She's the one who likes him, not the other way around. She should accept him as he is. But then, you never know, maybe she'd fallen out of love with him – she hadn't been paying much attention to him lately. It used to be different. He never saw her face to face, but he knew that she had her eyes on him: she'd sit behind him in the library and stare blankly at his back, as if in a trance. He asked her out, and they dated, but their relationship never went anywhere. They definitely weren't suited to one another. He was okay with this... But why did he so look forward to Thursdays? He hated university and would use even the tiniest excuse to skip class, sleep until noon, and spend the whole day online.

He turned off the computer. Soon his job would be

completed, and then, after receiving his fee, he could relax a little. Sleep normally. Or go out to a club, take some ecstasy.

Nearly asleep, he suddenly remembered that she was playing in a band now, and he felt bad that he didn't like rock or any other kind of hard music. Sometimes he'd say spiteful things about what she listened to, just to get at her. He regretted this now, but it was too late. He lay on his bed fully clothed and fell into a deep sleep.

He was, of course, late to class. In the hallway he saw a friend of his.

"Why haven't you gone in?" asked the web designer.

"Didn't make it in time," said the friend.

"Right."

"Want to get a beer or something?" The friend looked bored.

"Why not?" said the web designer. "I don't feel like doing much anyway."

They went for a smoke on the front steps. And then they saw her: she was walking very quickly, wrapped up in a scarf and out of breath. He smiled and wondered whether he should say hello. No matter: she didn't look up, didn't even glance in his direction.

To hell with it, he thought, but then for some reason he felt uneasy. And, like in a vision, he suddenly imagined giving her green roses. She'd said that was the only kind she liked, but he wasn't sure green roses actually existed.

"Is there such a thing as green roses?" he asked his friend.

The friend thought it over, then observed philosophically:

"Roses come in all colors."

"Even green?"

"Yes, green too. If you like, we can go to the Arch and have a look."

"Let's go."

A crowd of women with large buckets of flowers were hawking their goods at the Arch. "What would you like, young man? Something in special wrapping? Something for your girlfriend? Yes, those last a long time. And those – the "Angelika" brand – go on and take them, they're better than the Dutch ones. The Dutch flowers cost more too. No, those are Russian, they're ours."

"What are you looking for, fellas?" asked a ruddy-cheeked woman who had just pounced on them. She wore fingerless gloves and an enormous puffy anorak.

"Green roses," said the web designer.

"Yes," said the friend, "would you tell us what factory produces them?"

"What?" The woman blinked in amazement, then responded in an unsteady voice: "No, they're grown that way."

"Green ones?" The friend couldn't believe it.

"Yes, green."

"And how much would such a beautiful item be?"

"Seventy rubles. Per stem."

"And if I pay you more, could you repaint it orange?" the friend asked.

The woman realized that she was being mocked in the rudest manner possible and she scowled. The web designer and his friend roared with laughter as they went off.

9

Everyone I knew was at Korovin's party. I could barely breathe from all the smoke and could barely think from all the alcohol. I regretted coming. All the way to the center of town, and for what? Even though all my friends were there I felt miserable. Billy was there with that stuck-up girl we saw at Partisan; so were Genka, Kirill, and couple of other first-years, even the web designer, though it wasn't really his crowd. Then I saw him – my London guy. He was chatting up some other girl and smiling. I only hope they're not talking about London. Ah – Paris, of course.

"Hi," he said as he walked toward me.

"Hi," I said. I didn't know what else to say, everything I could think of was idiotic.

"How are things in London?" he said. "Setting off soon?"

I said nothing in return. I just left. By which I mean I left the party altogether, threw on my coat in the stairwell, and ran out into the street. A few minutes later he, my London guy, caught up with me.

"Did I say something wrong?"

"No, it's just that…"

"I get it," he interrupted. "I must've said something…"

We found ourselves standing very close together. I couldn't look him in the eyes so I looked the other way. We were near the circus where banners overhead advertised a travelling act of polar bears. I've hated circuses and clowns ever since I was a kid. A security guard appeared out of nowhere and watched us sternly.

"Let's get out of here," said my London guy. I followed him without hesitating.

We said nothing. He didn't even joke like he usually did. My head was in a fog. I was drunk, but not very. We walked quickly down Svoboda Street, past the McDonald's and the four-star hotel, past the park and the jewelry stores with their glowing alarm buttons, past a bank and a 24-hr food store. Apart from us there wasn't another living soul, just the occasional taxi speeding by. This made the city, so ordinary under the light of day, seem unfamiliar and full of latent danger. But next to him, my London guy, it was warm and peaceful. Suddenly I realized that I was smiling. I looked at him, and he smiled back at me.

All of a sudden he stopped in the middle of the street and took a hacky sack out of his bag.

"Want to play?

"But what about all these puddles?"

"Who cares?"

There under a streetlamp we began to play that ridiculous, pointless game. We kicked the sack, knocked it in the air, passed it from foot to foot, and then we were all played out. We sat on our heels and smoked. All the benches were still wet from the rain, but the air was clean and fresh. The streetlight went out. Dawn was near, but a pale strip of waning moon still dangled in the sky.

"This is good," I said.

"It sure is," he said.

Then we stood up and wandered on.

We reached the river embankment. On the way there we bought a bottle of champagne from a late-night stand, and we sat on a cold bench, drinking and looking at the Strelka. We got up and kicked the sack around again. We kept letting it drop, more often even than the first time, but we laughed about it. It all ended when morning came and the fountains were turned on. I still hadn't told him how much I loved him.

10

Kirill was always listening to music. Even after practice, when any extraneous noise would seem to cut into your ears, and the only thing you wanted was peace and quiet, he would still be listening to something. Kirill was music, and music was Kirill. They were bound for eternity. *I can't go on without you... you complete me...* or something like that. He was either listening to music or playing it. Which meant that Kirill never experienced silence. If it wasn't music, then it was some other sound: people talking, cars driving by, the noise of the city. When the city was in a good mood he heard street musicians playing on Kirov Street; trams clanking down the rails; a man known throughout the city for his powerful voice advertising an ordinary jewelry store; the inviting, upbeat ads for yet another film playing from speakers outside the central movie theater; skateboards scraping across Soviet Square; car horns blaring; and "Slavic Woman's Farewell" which was played every time a train departed for Moscow. But when the city was in a lousy mood, Kirill heard drunks fighting in alleyways; the squealing brakes of careless motorists; a distraught child who wasn't allowed to go on the carousel; the creaking of unoiled shop doors; old women arguing in line at the bank or the post office; the maddening sounds of someone's alarm system, workingmen swearing at the restoration site of some ancient building. These were the sounds he loved most of all.

He usually went home on the tram. There was a bus stop close by, but Kirill loved trams. The slowness, the rattling, the romance – he loved everything to do with trams.

Kirill was a drummer, which meant that people thought he was odd and unpredictable – no other reason was necessary. To his parents, friends, and girlfriends, it seemed like he lived in his own impenetrable world: the world of rhythm. He wasn't trying to be some brilliant, world-famous musician. All he wanted to do was play, and the band gave him that opportunity. And for that he was grateful. Some of his friends turned their noses up at this: "It's a girl band." Kirill rushed to their defense. "Have you heard them play? No? Then you'd better shut the hell up." He loved them all. Even Billy. He loved hanging out with the girls at someone's apartment drinking wine or going to a rock concert at Partisan. He loved just being with them.

Kirill loved Jack White, who could emit such astonishing sounds from his bass guitar, and he loved Mary White and her exceptional talent on drums. Not with envy, more like a faint sadness at the fact that he could never play like that. I'm okay, thought Kirill, I am, I'm fine. A fathomless melancholy struck his heart. This happened sometimes, and when it did he felt like hitting his head against the wall or crying, but then he would close his eyes and repeat to himself: "Everything is all right. I've got it better than everyone else!" But this didn't help much. Actually, it never helped at all.

Lenka. Beautiful, impulsive, spoiled Lenka. A princess. He didn't have a chance. It wasn't just that she was two years older, or even that he was a drummer in a rock band, and she didn't listen to that kind of music. They simply weren't a good match: that is, he wasn't a good match for her. From the very beginning he told her: "I don't need anything. I'm not asking for anything and I'm not going to. I just want to be near you." She magnanimously proclaimed: "Fine. But I need my freedom – don't get too clingy." "I won't," he said. He did try, but this tormented him. He let her do anything she wanted. He begged forgiveness when she was in the wrong. He gave her cigarettes and brought her coffee. He never hugged or kissed her in public because she didn't like it. Occasionally he would try to end this unhealthy relationship, and he would succeed. But only for a few weeks. She had no trouble enduring his absence. Were you gone that long? I hadn't noticed. He, however, couldn't take it. He couldn't stand being away from her so long. He would approach her between classes, each time in fear: Will she talk, or will she turn and walk away? And so it was, time after time. I don't want to love her, he thought. But he did.

Lenka had been a princess from birth. She wondered: Why should she, a princess, be going out with some lowly first-year who, to make things worse, plays drums in a crappy band? She wanted to be going to theaters and cafes, not spending ages at practice sessions. She ignored him in class and was trying to have less contact in general. Not because she was worried what others might think – she couldn't care less what they thought – but because she was thinking of herself. A drummer and a princess are definitely not meant to be together, simply because a drummer is not a prince.

All the same, Lenka would sometimes drop by during rehearsal.

"Will you walk me home?" she would ask Kirill.

"I can't right now," he would reply, disappointed.

"Does that mean you can't or you won't?" she said angrily and left.

And he, of course, would jump up, nearly knocking over his drums, and run after her. He would return a few minutes later, distant and on edge. Then he'd start beating his drums like a madman.

11

A lot happens in the spring: people fall in love, some get married; others simply enjoy the sunshine. For Larissa this spring marked the end of an entire era. It may not have lasted a lifetime, but it certainly carried a lot of meaning. The web designer was taking his final exams. So what? So long as he passes, he'll be all right. Once he passes that last exam and gets his degree, everything will be over. He'll leave the university forever, which means he will no longer be part of her life. That's why she came early today: to see him, maybe for the last time. At some point their paths were bound to cross. But what if he didn't recognize her? What if she got scared and turned away just to avoid saying hello?

She waited for the web designer on the first floor. But he still hadn't come down. She thought of how stupid and ridiculous it was for her to wait like this, but she couldn't bring herself to leave. It was like he'd just vanished.

When everyone had left she peeked into the office

of one the instructors and asked how a certain young man from a certain group had done on his exam. The instructor was old, but very kind. He searched frantically through his papers without even asking what business it was of hers. He had probably been young once, and desperately, hopelessly in love with some girl from his class. As he searched for the register, she kept saying "only if it's no trouble, I don't want to bother you, I'll be going," but he would not let her go. Finally, he looked up at her:

"Passed. With a C."

"He passed," she echoed back.

"Yes, he passed with a C."

As soon as she left the office she began to cry. Not because she was worried about him, not because she was disappointed by the grade, and not because she hadn't seen him today: she just began to cry.

The end of spring wasn't just warm: it was stifling. The city was covered in a dust that only rarely got washed away under heavy rains. After our sessions we would go to the fountains, sometimes the ones by city hall, but more often the ones by the children's theater, the same place where I played hacky sack with my Londoner. We hung out with the punks on Kirov Street, bumming cigarettes off people walking by; we went skateboarding by the St Ilijah Church; we talked with friends in chat rooms. We drank: Larissa had champagne, the boys had beer. We laughed and came up with all kinds of stories; we drank ourselves blind as we partied late into the night, until it was time for us to each find our way home. Sometimes we cast glances at couples walking by and envied them a little. We tried to convince ourselves that what we had was better. But was it really? It doesn't seem at all important now. The main thing about that spring was that we were so beautiful, so free, and almost happy.

PART 3: SUMMER

12

Drink tea and coffee. Listen to music. Forget about it all and feel nothing. Sleep. Look at the sky. Don't do a thing.

We were falling into a state of hopelessness. It was hot, and we didn't feel like doing anything. We even started to forget that we were in a band. We had only one lazy practice a week. In the summer people would disappear for days, weeks, even months at a time.

One day Kirill texted to say he couldn't make it, and none of us cared: we didn't feel like practicing anyway. We messed around a bit: I played the drums, making it up as I went, and Billy played the bass. Together we tried to pass for the White Stripes, but it wasn't long before we got tired of that and left to buy wine at the House of Bacchus, a liquor store next to the university. We sat with our feet dangling over the edge of the dirty, uneven stage in the auditorium, drinking wine from the bottle and talking about everything under the sun. Billy was drawn to the philosophical.

"Nothing happens like you want. Why is that? God only knows. Probably because we live in this world and not the one we'd like to live in. But we've got to keep going even if we're stuck in a rut. It's boring, but we've got to keep going. Nobody knows where we're going, or why. But we all keep going, or at least most of us. I'm still going, and so are you two. Of course, something good happens every so often, but it always comes at a price."

"Why is everything so unfair?" I asked. This question wasn't for anyone in particular. Even if you knew the right answer, it wouldn't change a thing.

"Because life's fucked up," said Billy.

"You got that right," said Larissa, smiling.

We went back to Bacchus, drank more wine, and then

wandered the city until dark. On those muggy summer days we weren't comfortable anywhere. There were too many people at our favorite places, too many people we knew and didn't want to see, too many people asking "How are you?" and "How's it going?", too many saying "We should get together" or "Where have you been?" We took the lesser-known ways on the outskirts of town where we wouldn't see anyone we knew. We'd bike there past abandoned hospitals and a grain elevator. And then, when it began to get dark, we each made our own way home in the summer night.

So that's how our summer was: stupid, pointless, lame. The only thing worth remembering was the Open Air concert at Spartak Stadium. The heat made both drink and music hit our heads harder. The sun shone brightly, and fluffy white clouds floated in the sky. We were a bit drunk. Some people were not just drunk but also high. The concert hadn't even started yet, and we kept checking the posters to make sure we'd gotten the time right. The stage was already built, and now people were busy setting up the equipment. Some people were sitting in the bleachers, but we went to stand closer to the stage.

Billy showed up with that girlfriend of his. She'd traded the black boots for sneakers, but that didn't change her appearance much. Genka seemed sluggish, not quite there. Kirill came with some friends, not entirely sober. There were loads of people. Even the lame, mainstream types we didn't want to see at all.

Everything was fine once the concert got started. We were happy: we jumped ecstatically to the music, sang ourselves hoarse, doused ourselves from bottles of water in the heat.

When it got dark, we left the crowd by the stage and sat on the grass on someone's spread-out jacket, straining to hear one another over the roar of the music. Nearby a little boy in a sailor's shirt was picking a scab off his knee. Children were throwing candy wrappers at each other. A warm wind was blowing.

The busses were still running, but we decided to walk across the bridge over the Kotorosl River. Our legs and throats were sore, but we kept right on singing. We watched the sunset from the roof of the still incomplete Chaika Hotel. Every year there were rumors that it was going to be torn down soon, but the Chaika, a refuge for grafitti artists, climbers, parkourists, various nonconformists, and lovers of adventure like us, was still standing after twenty years. "It'll outlive all of us," said Billy. No one, or at least no one we noticed, was there that night apart from us. We sat at the edge of the roof and watched the panorama of the city and river, drinking from a bottle of something or other. We laughed a lot.

And that was our life...

13

He saw Lenka unexpectedly. She was walking on the other side of the street with a couple of guys. One was very tall, the other slightly shorter. She was laughing about something. A sinking feeling in the gut, arms and legs turned to jelly. Kirill wanted to go jump off a bridge.

They'd had a fight three weeks earlier, and he, like a fool, had been upset the entire time. He just couldn't relax. He was calling her several times a day, but she was never home and her mobile number was always out of service. Obviously she'd forgotten he even existed, couldn't care less about him.

Enough. Kirill stopped and looked at her retreating figure. She wasn't like that. He knew for sure. His classmates and friends laughed at him, saying she walked all over him, that she had him whipped. They couldn't understand what he saw in her. But none of them knew what she was really like. A princess? Sure. But she was the only one who could look at him like he was the one and only man for her, who could so sweetly run her fingers through his hair and say such warm and affectionate things. They didn't know that it wasn't always him who came running back; they couldn't possibly know that she sometimes stood at his door, crying and begging him to open up, to look at her, to forgive her. And on the other side of the door, he also cried like a child because she was crying. And when she was about to resigned herself to leaving he would open the door, and their love would be as real as is possible in this world.

The web designer lay on his back and looked at the sky. The smell of roasting meat reached him from the lawn. There wasn't a cloud in the sky. He usually did the grilling himself and would never let anyone else do it. But today he was okay with it. He didn't care if it turned out well.

It was all over now, his time at university. Not that there was anything that great about it, nothing memorable. Or maybe just one thing. Her. But why her? It's not like she was the only girl that liked him. Far from it. Though she was the only one who looked at him like that. He would remember her not because he was in love with her but because she had been in love with him. Even if it didn't work out in their final year, even if they almost never saw each other, he still wanted to believe that she loved him like she used to. And that at some point, just because, he would give her green roses.

Small clouds appeared in the sky, and again the smell of the *shashlyk* reached him from behind the building. Someone called his name, but he was too lazy to get up and go to them, his friends and classmates, too lazy even to call back. He wanted to be alone, to think about her. These weren't the kind of fantasies he had of other girls he'd known. He enjoyed just dreaming about her. He closed his eyes so he could see her face again. Sometimes it came to him easily, sometimes not, but he was thinking about her.

Genka and I were sitting on his balcony and talking in the summer twilight. It was a long time since we'd been able to have a good talk. He talked about her, and I talked about him, my London guy.

"It's weird the way it turned out," said Genka. "In the winter she said, 'Let's just wait for summer in your bed.' I thought things really would be different this summer. But now it's summer, and what happens? She stops coming for no reason, same as when she started coming. She stopped calling. And there's nothing I can do to get her back. I can't do a thing until she makes the first move."

After that I told him everything. Not just about me: about Larissa and her web designer, and about the friend of the web designer, whose name was Misha, and who was my London guy.

We didn't say anything to comfort one another. We just talked about them, both of us talking in our own way about ourselves. But it made us feel better.

In the end we got thoroughly drunk and went to sleep in the same bed in our clothes. But for some time afterwards those tales of love were floating in the air like wisps above the empty Coke can we'd been using as an ashtray.

PART 4: AUTUMN

14

The trees rapped the windows with their branches, shaking their yellow leaves in disbelief, as if astonished to find us still sitting in the auditorium. I couldn't understand it myself. I tried to concentrate on the lecture, but my head was spinning, and the words on the blackboard blurred together before my eyes, all of this from the wine we'd drunk behind the building where all our course's declassified elements used to hang out.

I dragged my pencil over the sheet of paper. I was trying to come up with lyrics for a new song, but all of it was terrible.

Not long before the end of summer we started practicing again. And right after that was the greatest moment of our lives: through one of Genka's contacts we were asked to play a gig at Partisan at the start of November. This was more important than everything else: love, school, parents. We quit messing around and started practicing for real, often late into the night.

Sometimes fans would drop by during practice. Two guys from the year ahead of ours, both tall, but also kind of awkward. Nothing special, we said of them. They sat in the back row of the assembly hall and watched us. I doubt they were great admirers of our art – they didn't look like punk rock lovers – but it was flattering they were at all interested. Two first-year girls would come to see Billy. They traded secretive whispers in the front row. Billy would smile and wink, but then run off as soon as practice was over so he didn't have to talk to them.

Every so often the Princess would show up. We were all surprised at how calm and quiet she was: she didn't get upset or make a scene. During breaks she sat next to Kirill, but otherwise she spent whole evenings in silence, spinning one of his drumsticks in her hand. Kirill, pleased for some reason, would take a swig from his beer and laugh.

After everyone had left, Larissa and I would stay awhile. We'd sit on the filthy stage and drink wine, or we'd just talk. A long discussion every time, and always about the exact same thing.

15

In a small dimly-lit room with yellow walls, cluttered with boxes of God-knows-what, we were trying to calm our nerves before the concert. I was drinking champagne from the bottle,

Billy had wine in a plastic cup, and Kirill was drinking beer. Larissa was smoking. It was perfectly clear: we were all suffering from stage fright. On top of that, we were afraid to admit it to one another.

I didn't know if there were a lot of people there – I didn't peek into the room – but Genka had already run in to say, "Your public awaits." It would've been better if he hadn't said that, and better still if no one had been waiting for us.

All I've got to do is smile, I thought. But I went on stage twitching and morose. My hands trembled as I picked up my bass. Larissa, standing at the microphone, smiled nervously at me. I nodded back. I tried not to look past the stage, tried imagining that the room was empty. Larissa said a few words into the mic, but I couldn't hear what: my head was going in circles. And then we started. With the song "Rock'n'love." At first I wasn't too sure of myself, I made mistakes and heard the others doing the same, but after a while we started to get into it: we weren't that upset when we messed up and we played our hearts out. Sometimes Billy and I exchanged glances, and he smiled at me like a kid, and I could see from his face that things weren't going that bad at all. Larissa's voice had stopped quavering. It was amazing: being on stage, looking out into a packed room. I wondered: Where did all these people come from? Toward the end we played "Time of Your Life," with me joining in during the chorus, and then we finished up with our favorite "I Love Punk!" which the audience had requested as an encore.

After the show Larissa and I stood facing one another in the wings.

"We did it!" I said.

"Yeah!"

We drank again after the concert. Someone was congratulating us. I remember Kirill was floating, wildly happy. And Billy was kissing his girl in the black boots. Then we drank some more. We went into the main room and danced, jumping up and down to our favorite music.

16

She couldn't remember what happened: it seems she'd had a few too many. Nauseous. She leaned over the toilet, then pulled her head up and put her back to the cold wall. Again and again. Someone came into the bathroom: women's voices, but she couldn't make out who was talking about what. She couldn't stop shaking. Snippets from that evening flitted through the air. Until that moment Billy had always been close. And they kissed. She tried to think that it didn't mean anything. They were friends, and friends kiss sometimes, that's what she'll tell Billy next time. She's got to tell him that. But friends don't say they love you. That's what he said. Why did he do that? I can't stand him sometimes. She put her hands over her face and started to say: "Billy... Billy... Billy..." Her whispering turned into tears. Billy had always been close. She couldn't live without him. And she – didn't – need – anyone – else. Why didn't she realize this earlier?

Billy found her on the floor in the women's bathroom. Her mascara was running, her lipstick long faded, and her hair was all over the place. And still... still she seemed to him the most beautiful girl in the world.

"What are you doing on the floor?" He sat down and took her in his arms. "Let's go home," he said.

She moved his hand aside.

"Don't, Billy."

He waited a moment before talking.

"I'll just take you home and put you to bed, like I used to."

"Used to..." she mumbled. "We used to be friends."

"And we're still friends... my feelings for you... they... you don't need to know anything about them, understand? Don't even think about it."

"Why me, Billy? Why? I'm intolerable. I'm always whining and complaining, I..."

Billy again took her in his arms and smoothed her hair.

"Why would you say that? You're so wonderful, you don't even know how wonderful you are."

Tears welled up in her eyes: no one had ever said anything like that to her. She'd heard them say how beautiful she was, or "I want you so much", or "you've got a great ass", things like that, but no one had ever said such simple, beautiful words.

"Get me out of here, Billy."

17

He had a bunch of green roses in his hands.

"Hi," he said, smiling. "These are for you."

Every thought immediately left her head. There was nothing. Not him, not her, nothing good or bad, no past or future: nothing but her favorite roses. If she had been able to think at that moment, then she certainly would have thought: "How can it be? Someone must've told him... He couldn't possibly have guessed. He couldn't!" If she had been able to think, she certainly would have thought that, but as it was, every thought had left her head.

Then she didn't care at all how he knew about her favorite flowers. The important thing was that he was offering them. Him and those green roses. To hell with everything else. To hell with the entire world. And no matter what anyone said, she knew that she would never let him go. She would discover a new planet, learn to cook, take up a sport, build her own website, give up the band, cancel her phone, renounce everything in her former life, do anything and everything so long as he would be with her and only her. She realized this and smiled.

"Shall we go?" he said after giving her the flowers.

She wanted to ask what he had in mind and then say that she wasn't so sure. But then she suddenly realized that she didn't care. All that mattered was that he was at her side.

"Let's go," she said.

Epilogue: December

The band broke up at the end of December. We didn't have a plan, didn't set a particular day. It just stopped existing, and that was that. We had something of our own that we never could have had when we were together.

We were just looking for love. Punks, partiers, rich kids, hipsters, metal heads, wasters, junkies, neglected people with neglected lives, holier-than-thou girls, the beautiful and not-so-beautiful – everyone is always looking for love. Everyone wants this to break down barriers. To go to sleep and wake up with the same person, even if he's not there. But no one admits it.

Genka disappeared. Maybe he'd found a new girl. Or maybe not. I don't know. I'm just saying that it's been a long time since I saw him. And he still hasn't returned my Oasis CD.

Kirill left university to go to some music school in St. Petersburg, and it seems he's settled there forever. He never saw any more of the Princess, either. We saw her sometimes walking past with preppy boys who didn't look like Kirill at all. Soon after he left she approached me in the bathroom and asked where he was. I told her I didn't know and that I also hadn't seen him in a long time. She nodded and never asked about him again.

Billy and his girlfriend are still seeing one another. I sometimes have a cup of tea with them. They seem happy, but who knows what goes on behind closed doors.

Larissa and the web designer are living together and are about to get married and all that. She finds ways to tolerate him, and he finds ways to tolerate her.

And me? What about me?

Sometimes I see my London guy. I heard that he was married and had a daughter. We say hello and ask, just like normal, "How are things?" We say "See you later," and he rushes off to do whatever it was he was doing. And I smile because I remember that great time, when I was having the time of my life. Rock and roll, my first love, naïve dreams, freedom and youth.

Translated by Christopher Tauchen

Tales of the
Old Theatre

TALES OF THE OLD THEATRE

THE TALE OF THE ARCHITECT AND THE UNKNOWN ACTOR

Once upon a time the walls of the old Theatre had been painted yellow; now they were dull and worn, and most of the paint had peeled off. Cracks ran like wrinkles in different directions, and graffiti scrawls were still visible despite the feeble attempts to paint over them. The building wasn't actually that old, but its pitiful state made it look as though it had been there since time immemorial.

The Theatre was tucked away in a quiet spot in the centre of town, flanked by a city bank on one side and a shopping centre on the other. A lane lined with poplars and narrow yellow benches led away from the back of the Theatre. In spring the flowerbeds there were full of purple irises, pansies and wild roses; amorous young couples came here to stroll, and the benches were colonized by groups of teenagers swigging beer from large plastic bottles. In winter it was deserted, used only by actors and solitary pedestrians on their way home.

The Theatre's architecture combined features of neoclassicism and modernism. The building was modestly decorated but undeniably imposing, rather like a bashful maiden whose ignorance of her own beauty serves to enhance it. There was nothing ostentatious in the harmonious appearance of the Theatre, in its classical proportions and regard for the traditions of antiquity – just a great love of art, architecture and the theatre.

The façade and side walls were adorned with sculptures crafted from marble and stone and executed with reference to motifs from Ancient Greek tragedy. The portico featured a niche containing a group sculpture: in the centre, wearing a laurel wreath and holding a lyre, was Apollo, protector of the arts. To his right was Thalia, muse of comedy, and to his left was Melpomene, muse of tragedy. Both were pensive, melancholy and magnificent in their draped robes, which emphasised their breasts and thighs.

Inside the building, the foyer was cool and quiet; the floors were covered with coloured tiles, and the main staircase leading to the first floor was made of marble. The auditorium was decorated with a painted frieze depicting an ancient ritual procession: the muses, half-naked goddesses and long-legged, muscular deities danced and drank wine to the rustle of a red velvet curtain with a white tasselled fringe.

The Theatre was built in 19—. It was designed by a German architect who had been invited to the city of N by the Mayor. The architect was a modest and cultured man. Having suffered from a slight stammer since childhood he was not particularly at ease in social gatherings, but nevertheless he was well liked in the city of N. He had a sparse beard and wore a morning coat embroidered with roses, together with a pair of laced ankle boots. Although his personal style was considered highly eccentric at the time, it did not in any way detract from his artistic achievements.

While the Architect was working on the construction of the Theatre he inadvertently fell in love with a certain Actor, who was exceptionally good-looking in a classically Slavic way. The Actor's physical appearance made people assume that he was an honourable, strong and noble man. In actual fact he was capricious, egotistical and, as is often the case with beautiful people, exceedingly dull.

Occasionally, feigning reciprocal interest, the Actor would join the Architect for dinner or a walk. At the slightest encouragement from the Actor – a look, a word, a smile – the Architect would tremble and ask almost pleadingly, "D-d-do I h-h-have any c-c-cause to h-h-hope…?" The Actor would appear to nod his assent, but the very next day he would withdraw his affections, becoming cold and distant. He would go drinking in taverns and flirt with young actresses, but he always returned to the Architect a few days later. Again he would look at him with fluttering eyelashes, bashfully lowering his eyes as though he were passionately in love and blushing when the Architect touched his hand. He was playing at being in love out of boredom, for his own entertainment, not fully understanding that the Architect, who was accustomed to sincerity and openness, believed the whole charade.

In an attempt to sublimate his emotions the Architect devoted himself wholly to his work, but still he could not forget the Actor. Ultimately, he poured all of his suffering, his passion and his tenderness into the creation of the Theatre, and although his love for the Actor remained unrequited, and his work brought him neither fame nor fortune, he felt no regret.

As soon as the Architect's work was done he left for his homeland and never returned to the city of N. He left his heart in the Theatre, in an unfeeling edifice of stone, plaster and paint, which was destined to become not only his masterpiece but also one of the country's most renowned works of art.

The Actor's fate was less illustrious: a few years down the line he took to drink, stopped getting work and was soon forgotten. According to the gossipmongers it was no great loss to the Theatre, because as an actor he had been distinctly average.

The Theatre was also subject to the vicissitudes of fate.

It thrived in the early years, thanks to the patronage of the Mayor and the local administration. Attending a performance at the Theatre was considered to be worldly and fashionable; the repertoire included plays by Shakespeare, Ibsen and Chekhov. On some occasions demand was so high that extra chairs were placed in the auditorium. The company went on tour to other cities and other countries, and the Theatre hosted visiting troupes who came with their best productions.

Unfortunately, just before the elections, the Mayor died quite suddenly. His successors, who were not renowned for their integrity or any particular fondness for the arts, failed to allocate any funds for the maintenance and upkeep of the Theatre.

First the roof began to leak, then whole chunks of plaster began to fall from the walls. The curtain, once so luxurious, was reduced to rags – in some places burned, in others ripped. There was no money to replace the light-bulbs, so the corridors between the stage and the dressing room, the administrative offices and the other rooms backstage were dim and gloomy. New costumes were sewn from old, and the same props were used for three different plays. The Theatre was in dire need of renovation and had been for some time, but there was no one to take on the task and so a few years later it came to the end of its natural life.

Like many other buildings that fall out of use and into disrepair, at some point it will inevitably be declared a monument of cultural significance and awarded protected status. In fact, all that will happen is that the windows and the stage entrance will be boarded up and a heavy padlock will be hung on the front doors. A few years after that it will be turned into a hotel. By then no one will remember the cultural significance of this monument.

The Tale of the Artistic Director

Many years ago, Roman Nikolaevich – the Theatre's Artistic Director – had set up his office in a small room on the ground floor of the Theatre, next to the dressing rooms, and he had been there ever since. The middle of the room was occupied by a large desk, which was piled high with paperwork and figurines made out of papier-mâché. To the right of the desk, in the corner, was a cupboard full of documents; on top of this cupboard stood a plaster bust, nicknamed Van Gogh on account of its missing nose and right ear. To the left, next to the window, was a sofa, which was littered with newspapers, stage props, printouts of plays and discarded sweet wrappers. Roman Nikolaevich never tidied his office. He didn't have a secretary to do it for him, and the cleaner only dusted the surfaces and mopped the floors. In former times people had put the state of his office down to the idiosyncrasies of his creative, intellectual personality, but latterly his occasional visitors had begun to view it more as simply slovenliness.

There was a knock at the door and Ivan Timofeyich came into the room, without waiting for an answer. The Artistic Director abruptly shut the desk drawer and pretended to be writing something in a thick exercise book.

"Just a minute," he said, without raising his head.

Ivan sat down on a chair to wait. Roman Nikolaevich finally put his pen down and looked up. His chin was trembling and his face and eyes were red.

"Would you like some brandy?" he asked.

Ivan shook his head.

"Well, I'm going to have one, if you don't mind," said Roman Nikolaevich, taking a small bottle of cheap brandy from the top drawer of the desk. He drank straight from the bottle, pulling a face – there were no snacks to chase it with. "So tell me," he continued, "what's the matter this time?"

"Oh, the usual. We need new light-bulbs, we need plaster and paint... We need money, Roma."

"I see, and where am I supposed to get it from? You know as well as I do how much we made last month. It's barely enough to cover the salaries."

"We have to get it from somewhere. Maybe we could increase ticket prices, or ask the mayor's office? Surely it's in their interest to prevent the Theatre falling apart!"

"Oh, come on... Nothing would give the mayor greater pleasure! Imagine a plot of land this size becoming available, right in the centre of town – the perfect spot for another shopping centre! No, the mayor won't give us a penny."

"But you haven't even tried!"

"True. What's the point?"

"What's the point of anything?" asked Ivan, mimicking the Artistic Director.

"What do you want me to do, Ivan?" cried Roman Nikolaevich, raising his voice in a fit of temper. "You know better than anyone that I'm already doing all I can! Absolutely everything that is within my power! I've given my entire life to this Theatre, for God's sake! My wife left me, my grandchildren don't want anything to do with me, I'm half starving... But why am I telling you all this? What do you honestly think I can change? I can't force people to go to the Theatre! They don't need it any more."

Ivan Timofeyich couldn't argue with this. He had seen it with his own eyes – the stalls growing emptier by the day, groups of schoolchildren and students larking about in the boxes and the balcony, drinking hard spirits and cracking sunflower seeds. It would be better for everyone if they didn't bother coming at all, but educational establishments required their students to make a certain number of visits to the theatre.

Ivan Timofeyich could still remember a time when people came to the Theatre in evening gowns and smoking jackets, when nobody chewed nuts or swigged brandy from hip flasks during the performance. Back then the Theatre itself, as well as its Artistic Director, had been different.

Success had come easily to Roman Nikolaevich in his youth. Earnest and driven, he was barely in his thirties when he was appointed director of the new Theatre. The appointment was essentially a whim of the Mayor at the time, who had seen something in him – a passion, a kind of fire that seemed as though it would never go out. Roman Nikolaevich adored the Theatre; he adored the stage and the art of the theatre. He somehow always managed to select the right plays for the repertoire and had an infallible knack for hiring the most talented actors. He was also greatly respected for his ability to get on with everyone – not only the actors and directors but also the front of house team, the usherettes, the cafeteria staff and even the audience.

On New Year's Eve Roman Nikolaevich would dress up as Father Christmas and give the entire company gifts: sweets, chocolates and handkerchiefs. There was always a big party in the Theatre, and a lavish buffet with champagne and canapés.

But time began to take its toll. Fewer and fewer spectators meant less and less money. The troupe was reduced to a minimum, and the shortage of actors inevitably meant that the repertoire was pared down too. Roman Nikolaevich still dressed up as Father Christmas at the New Year's Eve parties but he no longer handed out gifts, and they weren't really parties – there were just a couple of bottles of champagne, bought by the staff themselves, who stood around listening to a drunken Father Christmas promising that things would definitely get better, and that next year everything would be fine.

Either out of the goodness of his heart, in recognition of their old friendship or as an acknowledgment of his eternal gratitude, Ivan Timofeyich followed the Artistic Director like a silent shadow – hiding the unfinished bottles, trying to pick the right moment to send him home and covering for him in front of the actors. The difference was that he no longer looked up to the Artistic Director.

He thought Roman Nikolaevich would cope, that he would manage to put a brave face on it and persevere against the odds, but then all of a sudden he seemed to grow old almost overnight and stopped caring about anything.

It happened later that week, perhaps on Thursday – the Artistic Director went outside and spent the entire day standing in front of the Theatre. The sky was overcast and it was drizzling. The passersby, as gloomy as the weather, were preoccupied with their daily concerns and walked straight past him. Roman Nikolaevich observed them closely, but not one person so much as glanced either at the Theatre or at the posters advertising the performances. The flow of people thinned out as the morning wore on – he saw a couple of schoolchildren, a group of students, two or three unemployed men... None of them looked in his direction either, although the students could easily have done so. One of the unemployed men was clearly not in any kind of hurry and even stopped next to one of the posters to light a cigarette. Lunchtime was busier. By then the rain had stopped and the sky had cleared, but people still walked past the Theatre without looking at it. They looked straight ahead, at the road, at their feet, at their watches, at their companions – everywhere they possibly could except at the Theatre! It was as though it simply didn't exist. Several times Roman Nikolaevich actually shuddered and turned round to check the yellow building was still there. He ate nothing all day and got soaked to the skin but continued to stand there until twilight came, until he finally understood that his time was over.

Raisa the wardrobe mistress walked into his office without knocking.

"The mice have been eating the sets again," she told him, calmly and impassively, in the same tone she would have used to tell him that the curtains needed washing or that it was raining.

The director reacted equally impassively to the news.

"Which sets?"

"The ones for *The Storm*."

"Well, the little blighters might as well enjoy them! We haven't staged *The Storm* for ten years anyway, and we probably never will again."

"Roman Nikolaevich..."

"Yes?"

Ivan could tell that another argument was about to start – the kind that would end up humiliating the Artistic Director, although he never seemed to realize it himself – and he leapt to his feet.

"I'll give you a hand, Raisa. Come on!"

Raisa stood there staring at Roman Nikolaevich for a little while longer, but she didn't finish whatever it was she was going to say. Instead she turned and left the office, with Ivan Timofeyich close behind her.

The Artistic Director put his head in his hands. He might even have shed a few tears. He knew that his colleagues couldn't stand him, but there was nothing he could do about that. He knew that his beloved Theatre was dying, but he couldn't do anything about that either.

Right now, more than anything in the world, he wished he were in one of the plays that he used to put on. Then he could have been sitting at his desk with a loaded revolver in the top drawer, like the one they had in the props – with a long metal barrel and a heavy black handle. Although this gun would be real. He would open the drawer, take out the gun, put it in his mouth and... BANG!

THE TALE OF THE WARDROBE MISTRESS

Raisa was in her fifties, but from behind she could easily have been mistaken for a much younger woman, what with her narrow waist, her slender ankles, her long, thick plait of lovely fair hair and the way she dressed. Raisa loved to wear patterned gypsy skirts, brightly coloured blouses and wide-legged trousers. Her arms were always adorned with multicoloured bracelets or bangles, depending on her mood, and around her neck she wore strings of beads, eye-catching pendants and long chains. Her ears were decorated with enormous hoops, clip-on costume jewellery, or clusters of multicoloured stones that fell to her shoulders. Full of exceptional optimism and sincerity, Raisa was one of those extraordinary women you find yourself instinctively drawn to. Within minutes of meeting her you were desperate to make a good impression, hardly daring to hope that you might become friends.

Raisa's extraordinary spirit was evident also in the world she had created in the wardrobe room. Pink stockings trailed from hats with feathers and wigs of all kind (auburn, blond, curly), topknots and false moustaches sat directly on top of shoes, instead of mannequins. Scattered amongst the chaos, which appeared to be out of control but was in fact perfectly well organized, were the costumes – all mixed together, historical and contemporary alike. The walls were hung with black and white photographs of famous actresses and scenes from various performances, and there was a little table with vases full of fresh flowers, from the garden of her dacha. Over by the window, in the lightest part of the room, once you managed to make your way through the ever-encroaching thickets of costumes and accessories you would find the most important item in the wardrobe room – Raisa's old sewing machine, which she had inherited from her mother. With the help of this instrument, she was able to create and effect extraordinary transformations.

Raisa and Ivan Timofeyich had been good friends for many years and might well have become lovers – both had failed marriages behind them, but their friendship meant so much to both of them that neither wished to jeopardize it. Even so, when he followed her to the storeroom where the stage sets and props were kept, Ivan Timofeyich fell back a step so that he could admire Raisa without her noticing – her beauty was so simple, so natural and obvious.

The stage sets for Ostrovsky's tragedy *The Storm* – bushes, a fence and a gate – were made out of cardboard and papier-mâché. They were already quite old and had been used for several other plays too, not one of which had been in the repertoire for some time. Ivan Timofeyich and Raisa had grown accustomed to doing things together, and so they worked instinctively and harmoniously as a team. He carefully held the sets while she applied glue and superimposed a new piece of cardboard, cut to size, then pressed gently to help it stick. They waited a while for the glue to dry, then found the right colour paint and diligently painted the new piece of cardboard until it matched its surroundings and looked almost as good as new.

Usually they worked in silence, but this time Raisa was strangely agitated and kept calling him by his diminutive name, Vanechka, which she never normally used. She talked about one thing after another – her dacha, work, the rain.

"What's the matter with you today?" asked Ivan Timofeyich, laughing gently at her bustling activity.

"Oh, I don't know. It must be these sets!"

"Why have they got you in such a flap? It's not as though it's the first time we've fixed them."

Raisa said nothing at first, then the words came tumbling

out, as though she were afraid that if she didn't speak her mind now then she never would.

"I tried to act the part of Katerina in *The Storm*, you know... It was a bad choice. Tragedy is not my genre! Whatever possessed me?"

"What are you talking about?" asked Ivan Timofeyich, confused.

Raisa smiled.

"I applied to drama school once."

"When? You've never told me this before!"

"There's nothing to tell. I didn't get in." Raisa sighed and was silent for a while. "I'm nothing like Katerina. I wasn't then, and I'm not now. Of course I had no idea at the time – I was young, I had my whole life ahead of me, and the dream seemed so noble, so attainable... But what did I know about anguish and suffering? How could I possibly understand heartbreak and a ruinous obsession with flight?"

As Ivan Timofeyich listened he imagined her as a young girl, tall and beautiful, walking into the main hall of the Theatre Institute. He saw two men and a woman sitting at a long table, sipping their water, making notes, calling "Next!" and looking up with interest when this cheerful, rosy-cheeked girl breezed in, because there was something special about her, something that caught your attention and made you look twice. She would have made a magnificent Governor's daughter in Gogol's *Government Inspector* but instead she read the part of Katerina, a character so alien to her, both physically and spiritually, that she convinced no one. No sooner had she begun the monologue about people not flying like birds than they said to her, "Thank you, that will do."

Raisa often thought of that hall when she lay in bed at night, unable to sleep. She imagined herself walking in and doing it all over again, but reciting something different this time, something joyful and impassioned. Her audience consisted of just three people, but they were the three most important people in her life at that moment, and when the hall rang with their applause she knew she'd been accepted.

"So that's what happened, Vanechka," she concluded. "As for the rest – how I became a dressmaker, how I married the wrong man – well, you already know all that."

Ivan Timofeyich couldn't find the words to comfort her. What could he possibly say? He took her hand and squeezed it. Just at that moment, a butterfly flew into the wardrobe room. Its wings were iridescent, a shimmering spectrum of bright blue, purple and turquoise. The colour of the sea. Neither Ivan Timofeyich nor Raisa knew that it was a *morpho rhetenor* – a rare species of butterfly found only in South America. Neither of them knew where it had come from or how it had found its way into this dusty room. Neither of them knew how long they sat there watching the butterfly in complete silence, captivated and entranced, until one of the usherettes ran into the room and the spell was broken.

"Ivan Timofeyich, there you are!" she cried from the door. "I've been looking all over the Theatre for you. Go to the hall, quickly, Lilya Viktorovna wants you – they need you on stage! I was supposed to fetch you straight away, but I've already spent half an hour looking for you. She's going to be furious!"

Smiling goodbye at Raisa, Ivan left the wardrobe room. The usherette ran after him, leaving Raisa alone with the beautiful butterfly.

THE TALE OF THE YOUNG PLAYWRIGHT

The actor who played the main part – the part of the Man – was late, and Ivan Timofeyich agreed to stand in for him in the rehearsal. All he had to do was read his lines from the script, although he already knew the part off by heart.

The play *Being Overruled*, which had been in the Theatre's repertoire for a number of years, was one of Ivan Timofeyich's favourites. It was a simple and touching love story about a middle-aged couple, who seemed to have grown apart. The husband spent all day languishing in bed, apparently suffering from "love-sickness", while the wife harboured a secret desire to sign up for acting classes and spent her time memorising Bernard Shaw's play *Overruled*. In reality, the husband had been jilted by his lover and the wife was too old to become an actress, but by force of habit they continued to play their respective roles. This play, by a Young Playwright whose name had long been forgotten, ran exclusively at the Theatre. The Playwright had refused to allow it to be staged in other theatres, having signed over all staging rights to Roman Nikolaevich.

This short summary of its contents would probably suffice, but the Young Playwright has his own tale, which is somewhat extraneous to our story but nevertheless deserves to be acknowledged.

The Playwright started writing plays at a young age and was convinced that this was his true vocation. However, his endeavours brought him neither fame nor fortune so he also worked in a firm selling men's shirts. From time to time amateur or student theatres would put on his plays, but this did not bring any tangible benefit and he continued to dream of seeing his plays performed at a real theatre.

"Writing a great play takes time," he would say. "A lot of time!" But he was able to find it only in short bursts – either in the bus on the way to work, or while he was taking a bath, or during his lunch break. Time was passing, but success remained elusive. His girlfriend was keen to get married, and she continually reproached him for his idleness and lack of commitment.

One day, having made the decision to take his future into his own hands, he announced to his friends and his girlfriend that he was going to lock himself up in his apartment for a whole year to work on a play.

"I'm handing in my notice, taking out all my savings and shutting myself up at home for a year. I'm not going to set foot outside, except to go to the shop or into the yard for some fresh air. I won't see anyone, not even my mother! I'll spend this time writing something – not just 'something', but something great! I'll sell it for a fortune, and then I'll finally be able to get married!"

This gave his girlfriend pause for thought. She couldn't wait to get married – she had her heart set on a big white dress, a pair of doves, a toast-master, a photographer and a reception after the ceremony at Canteen No.9. Everyone said the food there was excellent, particularly on special occasions. But on the other hand, if she waited just a little she could marry a genius! How her girlfriends would envy her then! So she agreed to wait for the Young Playwright.

After handing in his notice and settling a few other administrative issues, the Young Playwright was ready to embark upon his period of voluntary isolation. Not everyone is capable of tolerating loneliness, but the Young Playwright was actually looking forward to it. He anticipated the following schedule: he would get up at 8 a.m., go for a run, take a shower, have coffee and a fried egg for breakfast, then work on his play until lunchtime, after which he would permit himself a short nap. After his nap he would continue working, editing what he had written that morning, and then it wouldn't hurt to take a little light exercise. Finally supper, which would consist of chicken breast baked in cream, aubergine braised with mushrooms, salmon baked in sauce, fried potatoes with wild mushrooms or seafood spaghetti. He would permit himself a glass of wine with dinner, maybe two, and while he was eating he would listen to music. After dinner, of course, he would relax by watching a film or reading a book.

However, when he woke up on the first day of his new life, he felt like staying in bed a little longer. Why shouldn't he? He had the time, after all – a whole year's worth! And he'd been working so hard recently, he hadn't been getting nearly enough sleep. He eventually got up at around midday and sat down in front of the television. He wasn't in the mood to work – a filling lunch of meat dumplings had sapped his energy. When the infomercial he was watching ended (after he had given in and ordered a self-cleaning mop), the Playwright took *The Adventures of Sherlock Holmes* from his bookshelf and read it late into the night, snacking on sandwiches and sweet tea. On the second day, when his alarm clock woke him at 9 a.m., he remembered that he had stayed up quite late the night before and decided that he could probably permit himself a little lie-in. Again he slept until midday.

The third day was just like the second, as was the fourth, and so the weeks went by. The Young Playwright stopped shaving and no longer bothered to change out of his dressing gown, which by this point was in dire need of a good wash. When his food ran out, he would go to the nearest shop and stock up on dumplings, instant noodles and sandwiches, but apart from these rare excursions he never left the apartment. He put on weight and acquired an unhealthy pallor, but he neither noticed nor cared. At first the Playwright was in heaven – spending his days loafing about, drinking beer, watching television, reading interesting books, sleeping, eating, doing whatever he liked – but as time went on, little clouds began to drift into the clear blue sky of his existence, and these little clouds soon became storm clouds. He was almost out of time, and the play still wasn't written. Occasionally he would sit down at the computer and force himself to write a couple of lines, but lack of inspiration meant that he always ended up back on the sofa again. Every day he promised himself that tomorrow – yes, definitely tomorrow – he would be strict with himself; yet every day, when his alarm clock woke him at 9 a.m., he turned it off and slept until lunchtime. The storm clouds were growing larger and more ominous with every day that passed, and the Young Playwright wept at his own helplessness.

Then one day he came across the play *Overruled*. What was it about this particular play? What distinguished it from the hundreds of other plays that he had read that year? It is impossible to say. But whatever it was, as soon as he'd finished reading it he sat down at the computer and neither the television nor the self-cleaning mop could distract him from his work. Maybe his time had simply come. The play was written in about a fortnight, and the year was up ahead of time. It was not a great play, of course, but it was a good play – the best he had ever written.

The Young Playwright had a shave, put on a clean shirt and trousers, printed out the play on twenty-five sheets of paper and went round to see his girlfriend.

"Oh!" she exclaimed when she saw the Playwright on her doorstep. "I didn't think you were coming!"

"Why not? We agreed to meet in a year's time, so here I am. Ahead of time, in fact! What's the matter? Aren't you pleased to see me?"

"But... I didn't think you meant it."

The Playwright turned pale.

"Didn't think I meant what? What are you saying?"

"Well, I decided that I wasn't destined to marry a genius... So I married an electrician instead."

"But I'm not a genius," the Playwright said sadly.

There was a bench in the yard. The Young Playwright sat down on it, placing the pages of text on his knees. From that moment, the play that he'd been so proud of just five minutes previously ceased to hold any meaning for him. He glanced through it indifferently. Yes, it was good; yes, it was the best thing he'd ever written; yes, a real theatre might even stage it – but he no longer cared about any of it. Leaving the pile of paper on the bench, he stood up and walked away.

Five minutes later Ivan Timofeyich, who was on his way to work that day in good spirits, found some pages of printed text blowing about in the wind near his house and gathered them up.

THE TALE OF THE OLD ACTRESS

She usually finished work at 9 p.m. It took her until about 9.30 p.m. to get changed and then she would spend anywhere from a few minutes to half an hour chatting with those who were still at work, stretching the time out as much as she could to avoid going home. She left the Theatre between 10 p.m. and 10.15 p.m. and was home by 10.30 p.m. Without eating any dinner, the first thing she did was to take a shower. She would tie her hair up in a knot on top of her head, put a shower cap over it, climb under the hot streaming water and just stand there for several minutes with her eyes closed, not thinking about anything. Then she would take the citrus gel from the little shelf, squeeze it generously onto a sponge and rub it over her whole body – her chest, her arms, her legs, her stomach. She couldn't reach her back. After she'd rinsed off the soap she would dry herself with a large terry towel and then wrap herself up in it. She would rub cream into her face, take the shower cap off, let her hair down and comb it out. She would take an aspirin (or a glass of brandy, to help her sleep) and then lie in bed, flicking through the television channels and eating ice cream or chocolate-covered nuts. She would fall asleep to the sound of the television.

She was one of those ordinary, unremarkable women you can walk past in the street without even noticing. Something might catch your eye, a ridiculous coat or a shapeless lilac bag, but you don't bother turning round and a moment later you've already forgotten the coat and the bag, and as for the face – you never even noticed it in the first place. No one ever recognized her as the actress who spent years portraying the ravishing Nora in *The Doll's House*, the romantic Juliet in *Romeo and Juliet*, the loyal Lady Chiltern in *An Ideal Husband* and the enigmatic Woman in *Being Overruled*. All her ordinariness disappeared as soon as she stepped out on stage. It was the only place she could truly experience joy, suffering and death, and everyone believed in her.

Despite the popularity it had enjoyed during its heyday, the Theatre had always remained provincial in essence; consequently there was a high turnover of actors, particularly as far as the leading ladies were concerned. Actresses came and they went, in search of recognition and fame – some to bigger towns, some even to the capital – but they merely went from being stars in a small town to being anonymous and superfluous elsewhere. If they ever came back, life had worn them down to the extent that they were no longer suitable for the role of Juliet. Others got married and had children, and all of a sudden these charming leading ladies were transformed into ordinary housewives, with domestic concerns and family matters replacing the stage as the focus of their attention. Many promised themselves that they would return to the Theatre, but they never did.

Lilya was the only actress who stayed at the Theatre. She wasn't like the others. People advised her to leave – she could become famous, they said, maybe even a film star! But Lilya had no desire to leave.

Time passed too quickly. Without even being aware of it herself, she had stopped playing young girls in love and started playing their mothers. It was a strange feeling – the same plays, the same stage, but different roles. It wasn't that she'd made a conscious decision to devote her life to the Theatre, that was simply the way it had turned out. She had so many vivid, dramatic experiences on stage that real life seemed more like a series of rehearsals for a good play. The simple fact was that she belonged to a peculiar minority of individuals who don't strive for fame or fortune, and she was one of the lucky few who manage to find their place in life.

If she ever regretted not having a family or thought wistfully about the fact that she could have been a grandmother by now, then her memories of the roles she had played and all the emotions she had experienced on stage were on hand to comfort her, to stop her losing heart. The Theatre was her home and her family.

Moreover, she wasn't quite alone. She had a Devoted Admirer, who met her after every performance as he had in the past, in their youth. She hadn't found him attractive thirty years ago – he had seemed too young, too naive, too ardent – but the men she had favoured were now conspicuous by their absence. They had all disappeared. Her Devoted Admirer was the only one who had stayed, but by the time she realized that love and kindness are more important than certain other qualities it was too late. Back then she had been too young to value his devotion; now she was too old to make any changes in her life. Her face had become too wrinkled, and so had her heart. Or so it seemed.

But she did enjoy their evening walks. He was good company. And when she was with him, she felt that she became interesting and beautiful. She really had no idea why, but that was definitely how it felt. Yes, she could hold forth on any subject! She could keep up any conversation going! She was irresistible!

They could talk about anything and everything, with one exception – they never spoke about the future. It had already been decided for them. He mentioned it only once, when he had said to her that if he ever failed to meet her after the performance, if that day should ever come, it would mean only one thing – that he had departed this life. Although she didn't admit it to him, or even to herself, Lilya Viktorovna feared this day above all else.

* * *

She led the rehearsal as though she were the director of the Theatre – it wasn't the first time it had happened, and it didn't occur to anyone to contradict her. Even so the actors, relaxed by the absence of the leading man, were less than enthusiastic and began asking after just half an hour if they could make a phone call, or go for lunch, or run to the shops because there was a mid-season sale on. It didn't really matter... At the end of the day they all knew their parts, and in any case the prospect of stumbling over their lines in front of a dozen audience members, who probably wouldn't even notice, was not particularly terrifying. Lilya reluctantly let them go, one by one, until she remained alone with Ivan Timofeyich.

"The youth of today," she said suddenly, in the tone of Lady Macbeth, as she turned to face the empty auditorium. "They can't do anything! Just three hours of rehearsals! In my day," she continued, her voice trembling like Juliet's, "I could spend twenty-four hours a day on stage – the afternoon learning new parts, and the evenings performing. Where have those times gone?" she lamented, as doomed and despairing as Hamlet.

The actress froze, either lost in her thoughts or possibly playing a role, then she snapped out of her reverie and looked at Ivan Timofeyich.

"Are you still here? That's strange... You should have been the first to go."

"I can stay, if you like."

"No, you can go. Run along and get on with whatever it is that you do. I don't need you. Apparently there's a sale on in the shops."

"You shouldn't think of me like that," said Ivan.

The actress looked at him closely.

"I don't think of you at all. As I said, you may go."

He left, and Lilya Viktorovna stayed on stage, muttering her part under her breath. Though it might already have been a different role.

The Old Actress was not well liked in the Theatre. She was too arrogant, too bossy, and frequently sharp tongued. Only Ivan Timofeyich knew what she was really like. About a year ago he had been held up at work one night, and by the time he had finished the cleaning and his other jobs it was nearly 1 a.m. He left by the stage entrance, carefully closing the door behind him. Then, as he turned round, he saw Lilya Viktorovna. She was standing under a street lamp with her back to the Theatre. He could have slipped away unnoticed, but for some reason he couldn't bring himself to leave her standing outside in the cold. In any case he was curious to know what she was still doing there, when the performance had finished over three hours ago. He went up to the actress and touched her shoulder. She turned round, startled and somehow relieved, as though she had been waiting for this all evening... but when she saw who it was, her face took on its usual haughty expression.

"Oh, it's you."

"What on earth are you doing out here? You must be freezing! It's so cold. Can I walk you home?"

"No, thank you," replied Lilya Viktorovna, trying unsuccessfully to smile. "I'm just waiting..."

She clenched her fists, and Ivan Timofeyich looked at her as though he were expecting her to continue, to tell him who or what she was waiting for, but the Actress merely repeated, "I'm just waiting. Go home. I'll be fine. Don't worry."

Ivan Timofeyich, being the kind of person he was, couldn't help worrying about her. It was very late, after all.

"I can't leave you here like this," he said.

"Oh, what a gentleman," said the Old Actress, her voice dripping with sarcasm. She hoped that her tone would offend Ivan Timofeyich and that he would leave, but he ignored the jibe. She was a middle-aged woman, frozen and alone, and he had no intention of leaving her there on her own. She'd only spoken to him like that because she was feeling confused and emotional about something. It wasn't worth getting upset about.

"Can I wait with you?" he asked.

Lilya Viktorovna looked at him strangely and nodded. She had realized that there was no point trying to get rid of him. They stood there for a little while, with Ivan Timofeyich blowing on his hands and stamping his feet. He envied the actress and her endurance – she was standing perfectly still, without moving! Suddenly, more for his sake than her own (she knew that he would stay with her, however tired and hungry he was), she said, "Let's go home. It's late, and there's probably no point in waiting any longer. My place is not far from here. I'm quite capable of walking there myself, but if your chivalrous nature will not permit you to leave me here then you may accompany me."

Ivan Timofeyich nodded, and together they set out towards her house. He fell back a few steps behind her and didn't ask any more questions. He wasn't to know it, but that was the day that the Tale of the Old Actress came to an end.

THE TALE OF THE LEADING MAN

Although he wasn't hungry, Ivan Timofeyich went out to get something to eat. It was snowing, but the snow was melting away as soon as it hit the ground. No slush or dirty snowdrifts to worry about yet... But then, it was only the second time it had snowed that year. Ivan Timofeyich hadn't even got around to changing out of his autumn boots. In the shop next door to the Theatre he bought a bread roll and a packet of kefir, which he ate right there, in a sheltered spot called the Cafeteria, amongst the tall metal tables that were covered with breadcrumbs and spilled tea. There were no chairs in places like this, so he stood by the window and looked at the Theatre. The way the snow was falling on it reminded him of one of those glass balls with Christmas scenes inside, which you could shake and it would fill with snow.

Ivan Timofeyich seemed like an insignificant individual, but in fact in many respects he was indispensable. He had worked at the Theatre for many years, during which time he had learned how to do most things, such as cleaning the dark red velvet curtain, clearing the stage after every performance, changing lightbulbs and helping the wardrobe mistress mend ripped dresses. Neither he nor the Artistic Director who had taken him on could remember his original job description.

He hadn't been particularly popular with the girls when he was younger, and as he got older he became even less attractive. Being rather tall he had a noticeable stoop, which grew more and more pronounced with every passing year. His skin was so pale that it looked transparent and his hair, once dark and lustrous, had become lank and greasy. He had it cut every three months by an incompetent hairdresser. Unfortunately, neither of them seemed to be aware that the fashion for ruler-straight fringes had long since passed. Ivan

Timofeyich wore the same suit to work every day, although the dark blue, double-breasted jacket with large black buttons was slightly too small for him, as were the matching trousers, which rose up to reveal black socks emerging from the tops of his brown pointed shoes. In the winter, the jacket did its best to conceal a heavily pilled, dull grey woollen sweater with an indistinct pattern; when it was warmer, this was replaced by one of three shirts – either white with a dark blue stripe, lemon yellow for special occasions, or dark grey, which was the one he wore most often.

The first time Ivan Timofeyich went to the Theatre, he was taken by his mother – a strict, taciturn woman, of whom he was rather afraid. Ivan Timofeyich's mother considered herself to be a woman of culture. She went to concerts at the Philharmonic, although she didn't know a thing about classical music; she visited art galleries, but she knew little about painting; she pretended to read the Russian classics, yet she always had a paperback novel near at hand.

The sun hadn't yet set, but there was an early autumnal feel to the evening. From a distance it looked as though the Theatre had been dipped in gold. There were people milling about the front entrance wearing suits, snow-white shirts, bow ties, long dresses and high heels, their hair smooth and sleek. Some of them held flowers to give to the actors. Still just a boy, Ivan was completely charmed by the Theatre – he'd never seen anything like it.

He gazed in wonder at the mahogany railings surrounding the balcony and the dress circle, the chandeliers that were shaped like flowers, the painted frieze... He glanced secretly at the curtain and glimpsed a flutter of red velvet, a face peering around the edge, but then it immediately disappeared.

The second bell sounded, then the third. The lights gradually dimmed and then went out altogether. The noise gradually died down too, and finally the auditorium was silent. The curtain rose with a rustle.

His mother spent the first act looking forward to the interval – she decided that she would treat herself to a slice of sponge cake in the cafeteria, and perhaps even a double brandy. Being naturally insensitive and slow-witted, she couldn't comprehend her son's delicate spiritual constitution and didn't even notice the way he watched the stage, wide-eyed with awe. During the interval, while he was animatedly discussing the performance, she barely even listened. Tucking into a sausage roll, Ivan was saying how wonderful it must be to be an actor.

"Nonsense," declared his mother. "There's nothing wonderful about it at all. They spend every evening weeping and wailing, they don't have any personal life to speak of, they get paid peanuts and spend the whole year living hand to mouth!"

"But Mama..."

His mother didn't want to hear any more about it.

The idea of transformation – that was what he liked most about the theatre. You could be a beggar one night and a king the next. He could live a thousand different lives in that way. He could love beautiful women, the kind he could never dream of loving in real life. He could open himself up and lay bare his soul, but instead of contempt and derision it would be met with applause.

Every day after school he rehearsed different roles in front of his bedroom mirror. He read long monologues and poems, and he spent all his pocket money on going to the Theatre. Ivan's dream took him there every day, but real life conspired to hold him back. Although he knew that his mother would never approve of such an impractical choice of profession, he still approached her several times with the firm intention of telling her that he had decided to apply to the Theatre Institute.

However, his resolve always weakened under her glare. "I'll tell her later," he thought. But he never did. After school he studied at the Industrial College, and when he graduated he went to work in a factory. Deep down he already knew that he would never study at the Theatre Institute; not only that, but he wouldn't even try. He stopped going to the Theatre and began to avoid it altogether, so strong was his disappointment in himself, so great his envy of the actors. He decided to simply forget about the Theatre once and for all.

But some things are meant to be! It appears that people really do have a destiny to follow – their place in life is predetermined, and whatever they do, whatever challenges they may have to overcome, they find their own way there in the end. This is how it happened: they started laying people off at the factory where Ivan Timofeyich worked, and he lost his job. The day he received his final pay packet he walked through the checkpoint as he usually did, the heavy door closing behind him. He walked out through the main gates at exactly 5 p.m., as he had done for years, and suddenly he was overcome with a feeling of relief. Something had changed inside him. He didn't yet know that this was simply how it felt to be free. He didn't have a job or any money, but he was happy. The following day Ivan left the house, telling his mother that he was going to look for a job. He knew that he had a long road ahead of him. Up to this point in his life he had drifted along, doing what other people told him to, and even if he wasn't happy it had never occurred to him to do things differently. But now he was free to do whatever he liked, and his only fear was that he might not make the right decision.

It was no accident that he ended up at the Theatre that day, and it wasn't even fate – he knew exactly where he was going right from the start. Perhaps he had just wanted to prolong the suspense, to savour the anticipation of change.

After all, the feeling of expectation before a special occasion can be more enjoyable than the occasion itself.

Ivan Timofeyich joined the Theatre when he was twenty-five, and this story takes place when he was sixty-two. After working in the Theatre all that time, he could no longer remember being anyone else. Even his dream about the stage nearly came true.

He loved being at the Theatre late at night, when there was nobody else in the building and the main entrance was bolted shut. At night the Theatre's ghosts, all its stories and legends, came alive. Ivan Timofeyich knew them like his own and carefully safeguarded them, even when they were no longer any use to anyone. It was the only time he ever stepped out onto the stage and acted in front of a nonexistent audience, with a nonexistent cast. He had been doing it for many years and could no longer remember when it had started. At first he couldn't relax because of the feeling that someone was watching him; he was terrified of being caught, but after a while he lost himself in the role and forgot his nerves. Then he got used to it, and once he had established that he really was the only one in the Theatre that late at night his confidence grew. He would spend at least two hours on stage – the length of an average performance, excluding the interval and applause. Then he would finish his cleaning and go home.

* * *

Coming in through the stage door, he shook the swiftly melting snow from his boots and went straight to the auditorium, in the hope that they would have started rehearsing again. But there was no one on stage. So Ivan Timofeyich started dressing the set. The sofa he dragged out from the wings was old and ripped in places, with springs sticking out. Raisa had recently covered it with a throw, which was someone's old shawl. He added two cushions that had been decorated with appliqué work, apparently to brighten them up a bit but in actual fact to cover up the holes. Next to the sofa he placed a side table and a standard lamp. Ivan Timofeyich made a point of putting a new light-bulb in – the old one had gone out at the most inconvenient moment, in the middle of a performance. The only thing left was a tall, decorative mirror with several drawers in the base, but he couldn't manage that alone. Someone would come and help him sooner or later, but for the time being he had other jobs to be getting on with. All the little things he did – such as changing the light-bulbs, sweeping the floor in the cafeteria, emptying out the ashtrays in the men's toilet, putting bottles of water in the dressing rooms – might have gone unnoticed, but if Ivan Timofeyich hadn't taken care of them all every day, so thoughtfully and diligently, it is hard to imagine what might have become of the Theatre.

At around 6 p.m. the actors started drifting back to the stage. Ivan Timofeyich also happened to be there – he was cleaning the curtain and waiting for something, although even he didn't know exactly what.

"Something" appeared at 5.55 p.m. in the form of Roman Nikolaevich, out of breath and in despair. He reeked of brandy and bewilderment.

"I'm sorry everyone, it looks like we're going to have to cancel the performance after all. It's nearly six, and there's still no sign of Lev. If we hurry up, we might be able to find the money to refund the tickets."

Wearily, having reconciled himself to fate some time ago, he sank into a chair and covered his eyes with one hand.

"What are you talking about, Roma?" asked Lilya, her voice harsh and strident. "Why can't we just replace him? He'll do," she said, prodding a young actor, who had only joined the Theatre two years previously and hadn't yet been given a lead role. "He's a bit young for the part, but we can make him up to look older... The audience aren't exactly going to notice. They never usually do."

"But I don't know the part!" said the young actor.

"What do you mean, you don't know it? Who's Lev's understudy?"

"He doesn't have one," the Artistic Director said quietly. "He's never missed a performance. So there didn't seem any point—"

"Nonsense! How can you not have an understudy? Roma, what's the matter with you? That's completely..." Lilya trailed off, without finishing her sentence. "Do any of you know the part?" she asked, appealing to the actors, who had somehow instinctively huddled together in a group. No one spoke. The silence was saturated with the Artistic Director's dismay, the young actor's humiliation and Lilya's contempt, which further heightened the tension, but suddenly it was broken by the voice of Ivan Timofeyich. He heard it and thought it sounded strange – it must have been someone else, someone nearby, because surely it can't have been him speaking in such a high-pitched, squeaky voice. The voice said, "I know the part. I know it off by heart."

The Artistic Director, Lilya and the other actors stared at him in silence, as though a bedside table had suddenly announced that it wished to be an actor. People aren't generally given to conversing with bedside tables, so nobody spoke – not even Lilya, who usually had something to say.

The first person to speak was the young actor, who was motivated not by the desire to come to Ivan Timofeyich's rescue but by the desire to save himself from the sharp tongue of Lilya Viktorovna.

"Actually, it's not a bad idea... He often helps me rehearse, and he reads quite well, almost professionally! He'll be fine. You heard him yourself, today at rehearsals. Not bad, is he?"

No one else said anything. The other actors, all of whom had worked at the Theatre for a long time, found the idea strange and incomprehensible. They just couldn't imagine sharing the stage with someone who had no experience and was completely unprepared. How could he possibly know the part? It would be easier just to cancel the performance! Sensing a way out, the Artistic Director was delighted at the turn of events but refrained from expressing his thoughts aloud – the others might not agree with him, and he was too mild and indecisive to champion his own cause.

In the end Lilya Viktorovna decided on behalf of everyone, including the Artistic Director. "Go and get changed," she commanded. "If the costume's too big, ask Raisa to adjust it. Just do it quickly! We'll have to have a quick rehearsal."

Ivan Timofeyich hurried to the dressing room, unable to feel his legs under him. Everything around him was spreading and blurring like fog. He could no longer feel his own body and cursed his tongue for blurting out such nonsense. He was bound to bring shame on the Theatre! He didn't know how to act and had certainly never done it for real. "You fool, you fool," he muttered to himself, over and over again.

The first thing he noticed when he found himself on stage was that he couldn't see the audience at all – he was blinded by the stage lights, and the auditorium looked completely dark. In fact, he preferred it that way as it helped to calm his nerves. Gradually his eyes got used to the bright lights and he could see the audience, but as a single, communal entity rather than individual figures or faces. Suddenly his fear evaporated and he was no longer Ivan Timofeyich, but a lovesick middle-aged man.

* * *

When it was over, he felt like himself again. He stood there, surrounded by his favourite people, and he could finally see into the auditorium: it was full of people giving him a standing ovation, and his mother was sitting in the front row. He was sharing the stage with Roman Nikolaevich, Lilya, Raisa and the young actor, and they were all smiling. He was no longer a middle-aged man but seventeen years old, the age he had been when he wanted to leave home and become an actor, and everything still lay ahead of him – a whole life on stage, and so many parts to play.

THE LAST TALE ABOUT THE THEATER

A man wearing overalls and carrying a toolkit stopped in front of the old Theatre. He'd never been inside, although he'd heard a lot about the Theatre and the shows they put on. He hadn't heard so much about it lately, come to think of it, and he probably would have forgotten about it altogether if it hadn't been for this job.

The man went in and found himself in a cool, quiet foyer with posters on the wall. The ticket office was closed. The little number tags in the cloakroom were hanging on their pegs – all except one, which had been replaced by a man's overcoat. The whole place was deserted.

He walked down the corridor towards a door marked Staff Only, but the door was locked. He looked into the cafeteria and the toilets, but there was no one there either.

"Hello! Did someone call an electrician?" he called, feeling extremely self-conscious.

It was dark and quiet in the auditorium, but the man sensed that there was someone on stage.

"Hello," he began. "You called an electrician yesterday... I'm afraid we got held up, couldn't come any earlier... It was quite late when you called, to be honest, as we told your director..."

But apart from the indistinct echoes of his own voice, there was no reply. The man walked up to the stage... and then he stopped.

On stage, surrounded by props and sets, lay a man. His body was twisted in an unnatural pose, his eyes were staring out into the auditorium and his lips were frozen in a smile.

The post mortem revealed that Ivan Timofeyich had died of a heart attack. His heart had simply stopped beating, and there is a good chance that at least in his last moments he was happy.

Following this event the Theatre closed down, initially for an unspecified period of time and then for good. Like many other buildings that fall out of use and into disrepair, it might have been taken over by tramps and local teenagers, but before this could happen it was declared a monument of cultural significance and awarded protected status. In practical terms, this simply meant that the windows and the stage entrance were boarded up and a heavy padlock was hung on the front doors.

For a long time, everything inside the Theatre stayed the way it had been left. Organized chaos reigned in the wardrobe room: pink tights still trailed from hats with feathers, curly wigs still sat on top of shoes, costumes were still strewn about the room.

The Artistic Director's office remained home to official documents and diplomas, although they were covered with so much dust that it was no longer possible to make out the names of the recipients and what they had done to deserve them. A newspaper lay on the desk amongst all the papers and second-rate plays, open at the last article ever written about the Theatre.

On stage the curtain was still up, as though the performance were about to start. A pair of opera glasses lay abandoned in the fourteenth row of the stalls, seat number seven. Portraits of actors and actresses lined the foyer. All the little number tags were hanging in the cloakroom on the right hooks – except one, which had been replaced by a man's overcoat.

The posters near the ticket office in the foyer advertised *Decameron* on Wednesday, *The Honest Adventurer* on Thursday, *Two Funny Stories about Love* on Friday, and *Being Overruled* on Saturday. Unsold tickets for these performances lay in the ticket office. It was as though the Theatre were simply waiting for the audience to come back, for the actors to take to the stage, for the three bells to ring, the lights to go down and the performance to begin...

Several years later the Theatre was turned into a hotel. It's hard to imagine a Theatre being turned into a hotel, but that's exactly what happened. No one even remembered that the Theatre had been declared a monument of cultural significance. All that remained of this renowned work of art was the façade, and these tales... Tales that will never die but will in time become legends, like the Old Theatre itself, the memory of which will remain forever in the hearts of those who worked there and its audience.

The Artistic Director took to drink, and no one ever knew what became of him. Raisa carried on sewing, though no longer for the Theatre, and she raised two lovely granddaughters, hoping that one of them would become an actress. Lilya moved to another town to act in another small theatre, and she was never really happy about anything.

No one ever found out who called the electrician. As it turned out, there was nothing wrong with the electricity in the Theatre that day.

Translated by Amanda Love Darragh

GLAS TITLES ALSO AVAILABLE AS E-BOOKS

AVAILABLE FROM AMAZON & OTHER MAJOR PLATFORMS